MW00874743

1/10/95
0 circo
oo of 9/95

# Nothing Grows Here

JEAN THESMAN

# Nothing Grows Here

HarperCollins*Publishers*

Library of Congress Cataloging-in-Publication Data
Thesman, Jean.
  Nothing grows here / by Jean Thesman.
     p.    cm.
  Summary: When her father's death results in the loss of her house and garden
and a move into a shabby apartment house, twelve-year-old Maryanne adjusts
with the help of new friends and a new garden.
  ISBN 0-06-024457-7. — ISBN 0-06-024458-5 (lib. bdg.)
  [1. Moving, Household—Fiction. 2. Apartment houses—Fiction. 3. Death—
Fiction. 4. Gardens—Fiction.]    I. Title.
PZ7.T3525No   1994                                                93-45739
[Fic]—dc20                                                          CIP
                                                                     AC

Typography by Elynn Cohen
1   2   3   4   5   6   7   8   9   10

First Edition

*For my mother,*
*who taught me everything about hyacinths*

*Why stay we on the earth except to grow?*
—ROBERT BROWNING

# Nothing Grows Here

# Chapter One

"Five million neighbors are watching us," I told Mom.

My mother glanced up at the Aristocrat Arms, where several people gawked over their balcony railings at us.

"If they're laughing, don't tell me," Mom muttered. She bent into our dusty van and yanked at the shabby old love seat we'd hauled home. "This is hopeless, Maryanne. It's stuck. Everything we try just wedges it in tighter."

I gave one last disgusted look at our audience and said, "Well, that man who sold it to us got it into the van, so there must be a way to get it out."

Mom straightened up, sighed, and attempted to comb her tangled curly hair with her fingers. "We won't budge it without dynamite. I'm going inside to find somebody to help us."

"Mrs. Eldrich?" I asked doubtfully. Mrs. Eldrich, the apartment house manager, was an acquaintance of a friend of the sister-in-law of Mom's cousin Regina, our only relative. A week before, she'd hired Mom as a part-time housekeeper in the building, and we would get rent credit for her work. Mrs. Eldrich turned out to be absolutely horrible, but we were broke, so Mom couldn't quit. Not this soon, anyway. She'd been looking for work, any kind of work, for months.

"I'd rather die than ask for help from that ugly, meanspirited, nagging, whining—" Mom began.

"I get the picture, Mom," I said. "She's your best pal and you're going to start dressing alike." Both of us laughed. We'd learned one thing in the year since Dad had died—when everything else fails, try laughing. Maybe it will keep you from screaming.

I looked up at the apartment house again. All the heads had disappeared, probably because they'd heard the words *ask for help*. "Nobody's volunteering to give us a hand," I said. "Nobody's even cheering us on anymore."

Mom punched the love seat, as if that could have done any good. A small puff of dust rose. "Maryanne, in a neighborhood like this, nobody wants to get involved in anything, in case there's some loose blame floating around that doesn't have an owner yet."

It was August in Seattle, late in the evening of a day so hot that everybody lucky enough to have a choice had gone to one of the beaches. We had no choice, since we didn't have much furniture and had to spend Mom's free day prowling flea markets and yard sales, looking for the things we needed.

Just then a boy I recognized strolled out the door, acting as if he owned the place. I'd seen him hanging around the lobby. He looked about my age, twelve, and he was taller than I, with straight blond hair hanging in his gray eyes. He swaggered a bit, his thumbs hooked in his belt.

"Greetings and salutations," he said. "You people are in the no parking zone."

Who did he think he was? Greetings and salutations? "Go away," I told him. "We'll park wherever we want to."

"Sure, but not in the no parking zone." His round light eyes studied the van and the love seat. He seemed to have no intention of leaving anytime soon.

"I'll pay you to help us," Mom said briskly. "Never mind where we're parked."

"Deal," the boy said. He reached into the van and tugged at the love seat. It didn't budge. "I was watching you, and what you did was turn it too far sideways."

"Well, thanks for telling us!" I cried, exasperated. I was embarrassed to learn he'd been part of our audience, and the blue print love seat that had looked acceptable in the former owner's garage now appeared hopelessly threadbare.

Actually, it looked as if it belonged in the Aristocrat Arms, or across the street at the building's equally seedy double, the Executive Arms.

"I'll get somebody to help," the boy said, and he shot off into the building.

"Great," I said crossly. "Idiot." I sat down on the curb and wiped my forehead on the sleeve of my T-shirt.

"Do you know him?" Mom asked. She sat beside me and examined a broken fingernail.

"I've seen him in the lobby," I said. "His name's Tom. I've heard his little sisters yelling at him."

Mom laughed suddenly. "One is called Monica, I bet," she said. "Monica Kingsley. She's got an attitude problem, too."

Unwillingly, I laughed along with her. "Monica's the one who wants money to let people ride the elevator," I said. "I hope he doesn't bring her back."

But Tom came back with a girl my age. "This is Lottie Hale," he said. "She came along to find out if you're going to our school and what kind of clothes you've got." He directed this last statement, along with a snicker, at me.

"You are such a complete jerk," Lottie told Tom. "Don't you know how to introduce people?"

"I'm Maryanne Russell," I said as I gave this Tom my deadliest dirty look. "And this is my mother. We're glad to meet you, Lottie." I was miserably aware of my wrinkled shorts and soiled shirt. I hoped for an instant that the building would fall on me—as well as my tacky furniture.

"I've seen you around, Maryanne," Lottie said. She had blue eyes like me, but that's all we had in common. She had shiny red hair, while I had a thick tangle of dark tight curls pulled into a ponytail. She had more freckles than I did, but on her they looked good. And she was wearing a gorgeous—and clean—yellow dress.

"You're Margaret's daughter," Mom said suddenly, grinning. "I recognize the hair."

"Are you Beth?" Lottie asked. "The new slave?"

"Hey, are we going to move this couch or what?" Tom asked. Obviously he wouldn't let any conversation last long unless he was part of it.

"We'll move it in a minute, Tom," Lottie said. "What grade are you in?" she asked me. "Seventh? You'll be going to Maple Avenue Middle School then."

That put an end to one of my major worries. Now I'd know somebody when I started the new school in a few days. I'd gone to the same suburban school with the same people since kindergarten, and wasn't sure I knew how to make friends from total strangers.

With a big, melodramatic sigh, Tom climbed inside the van and pushed hard against the love seat. Mom, Lottie, and I took the hint and pulled on it. It moved a little.

"The furniture we had in our house was too big for

the apartment, so we had to get different things," I told Lottie. Then I hated myself for explaining. Lottie didn't need to know why Mom and I were out here, struggling with a piece of used furniture at seven o'clock on a hot Thursday evening.

"So did we," Lottie said. "Gee, this is a pretty love seat. Is the rest of your living room furniture like it?"

"No," I said vaguely, pretending great interest in the dusty geraniums in the nearest flower bed. We didn't have any other living room furniture, except a television set. We'd spent most of the day finding and hauling home a kitchen table and chairs.

At last the love seat popped out of the van and teetered on the curb. Breathing hard, Mom and Tom picked it up and carried it toward the building while Lottie and I ran ahead to open the door.

"You'd better open the elevator, too!" Tom called out.

Lottie and I hurried inside the lobby. She poked the elevator button and the doors slid open immediately.

Eight-year-old Monica Kingsley stood inside, like a troll in a cave. "Gimme a dollar or you can't ride the elevator," she said. There was a rim of chocolate around her mouth and a long rip in her shirt.

"Your mother told you to stop doing this, you brat!" Lottie cried.

"If you want to use the elevator, pay me," Monica said, blocking our way with outspread arms.

I'd had enough of Monica right after we moved in,

when she'd tried the same thing. "Get out of that elevator right now!" I yelled. "We aren't kidding."

"Jeez," Monica said. "Are you always this crabby?" She whirled around suddenly and ran her hands across all the buttons on the panel, then skipped off down the hall without looking back.

Lottie sighed. "Darn her. Now it'll stop at every floor. She's really awful, but her little sister Audrey is nice. And so is Tom, once you get used to him."

He's *weird*, I thought, but I smiled automatically. I hadn't known anyone long enough yet to comment.

The love seat barely fit into the elevator, and there wasn't much room for people to accompany it to the fourth floor.

"Run up the stairs with the key," Mom told me. "Tom, you stay with the love seat. I'll move the van before it gets towed away."

"We could ride the service elevator in the back hall," Lottie said, "but the stairs are really faster."

The stairwell smelled of frying onions and fish, and I was sure I could hear every TV in the building. I'd hate to invite a friend to come home with me here, I thought as I started the long climb. For the first time in my life I was ashamed of where I lived.

"Mrs. Eldrich hates it when tenants move furniture in the front elevator," Lottie said. "Actually, she hates everything the tenants do. Have you met Martie yet? Her exceedingly ugly and evil daughter?"

"Mom mentioned her," I said. I didn't want to meet

Martie because of the things Mom had told me about her, but I knew I'd have to, sooner or later. She was twelve, too, and we'd probably have classes together.

"There aren't many kids our age here," Lottie said. "Most of them are lots younger."

"Are they all like Monica?" I asked. I was grinning.

"You mean are they brats?" Lottie asked. She wasn't grinning. "Actually, yes. You'll get used to it, though."

Privately I thought Mom and I weren't going to be around long enough to bother getting used to it. Something good would happen. We'd get a break, finally.

When we reached our apartment we saw Mom and Tom staggering down the hall with the love seat. I unlocked the door, and my cat, Jimmy, leaped at me.

"What a great cat," Lottie said. "He's huge."

I stroked Jimmy's soft yellow fur and rubbed my face against the top of his head. "He misses having a yard, and we're afraid to let him out on the balcony because he might fall off."

"There's too much traffic on the streets around here to let a cat run free," Lottie said. "He'll learn to go without a yard."

No, he won't, I thought. And neither will I.

My mother and Tom put the love seat down. "Let's leave it here," Mom said. "Not that we could put it anywhere else, at least until we've got all these boxes unpacked."

"Can I help you put things away?" Lottie asked.

Mom groaned. "If I could find a place to put this stuff, I would. We don't have much closet space."

"Nobody does," Lottie said. "We use unpacked boxes for night tables and window seats."

"Thanks for the idea," Mom said. "I knew there had to be a solution."

Lottie told me she'd drop by the next day, and then she left, dragging Tom with her. He had unashamedly accepted a dollar from Mom for his help, even though Lottie had refused to take anything.

"Good night," Tom called out to me. "Farewell, cheerio, so long, and good-bye."

"Good grief!" Lottie cried. "Shut up, Tom, or I'll smack you."

Let *me* do it, I thought, scowling as I closed the door behind them. Any boy could be a pain, but Tom was a major aggravation. But at least I knew him. Now he was more than a stranger flashing across the lobby or pedaling quickly away down the street, dodging cars.

"Lottie seems nice, like her mother," Mom said. "I don't know how Margaret stands it, working for that Eldrich witch. But she loves her other job."

I bounced a little on the love seat. Jimmy purred, enjoying the ride. "Where else does Mrs. Hale work?" I asked.

"In the espresso shop on the boulevard," Mom said. She took two glasses from the crowded kitchen cupboard. "Lemonade, Maryanne?"

I moved to the secondhand table we'd found at a flea market in north Seattle. "How long have Lottie and her mother been here?" I asked.

"A couple of years," Mom said. She poured lemonade and handed me a glass. I held it against my hot forehead for a moment.

Two years was a long time to be stuck in a place like this. Of course, we'd get out before that. Something would come up. We'd find a place in our old neighborhood, and I'd be with my friends again. My life would be almost the same as it was before the hard times began, before Dad's electronics store failed. Before he got sick. Before he died.

Two years, I thought. I couldn't stand this place for two years.

"Hey," Mom said. "Everything okay?"

I blinked. "Sure," I said, swallowing tears. "Everything's fine." I never let Mom see me crying, not after those first awful months.

"Good," Mom said. "I'll have another day off on Sunday, so let's keep our fingers crossed that we'll find two dressers, and a coffee table, and who knows what else?"

"We won't need bedside tables," I said. "We've got boxes we can't unpack, so we can use them to put our stuff on."

"Hey, you're right," Mom said. She clicked her glass against mine. "We're going to make it, Maryanne," Mom said. "You just wait."

But Jimmy was weaving between my feet, complaining. I hate this place, he seemed to say. It doesn't feel right. I want to go home. I want things to be the way they were before the bad times came.

Later, in my bedroom, I closed the curtains to shut out the view of the run-down Executive Arms across the street. In our house, my bedroom windows overlooked trees and the garden Dad and I had planted. Views were important to me.

I sat on the edge of my bed with Jimmy in my lap. There was something I'd never told anyone. Sometimes I forgot Dad was dead—just for a moment or two. Sometimes, for a second, I'd panic, wondering what he'd do when he came home and saw other people in our house. How would he find us—if the whole thing had been a terrible mistake and he wasn't dead after all?

He'd be lost out there somewhere, looking for us.

That night I had a nightmare about being lost myself, and I woke, ready to shout, "Dad!" until I realized where I was. There, in the strange apartment that was now home, I hugged my knees to my chest. This couldn't last forever. We'd find a place that felt right, like a real home.

And I'd quit imagining Dad was lost in the dark.

I slid out of bed and turned on the light. Quietly, carefully, I opened my closet door, took out a shoe box, and carried it back to my bed. Then I took my unicorn music box off the windowsill and set it on the bed, too. It was the last Christmas gift Dad had given me. I couldn't wind it now, in the middle of the night—the music might wake Mom. I didn't want her coming in to check on me and seeing the shoe box. But I liked having the unicorn's company when I went through the box.

I took out eleven snapshots of our house and the acre surrounding it, the gardens and fruit trees, the lawn swing Dad had built, and the small pond he and I had dug ourselves. None of the photos had people in them. I kept those in an envelope and never looked at them because they always made me cry.

One by one I studied the photos. I traced my finger along the trunk of an apple tree, captured forever in full bloom. I spent several minutes looking at the snapshot of the back of our house, taken after a snow-storm.

Do the new owners take care of the yard? Do they remember to feed the goldfish in the pond?

I put the snapshots away and closed the box. While I'd been lost in the past, Jimmy had sneaked inside the closet and curled up to sleep on my old boots.

"Come on out," I told him. "You can't stay in here."

But he ignored me, and I had to crawl in after him, ducking under my clothes. When I picked him up, he squeaked in protest.

"Bad kitty," I whispered.

And then I saw the writing on the back closet wall,

so close to the floor I'd missed it when I was putting my clothes away after we moved in.

I HATE THIS PLACE.

Someone had written the message in a place where it might never be seen. But who? I hadn't given a thought to the people who had lived in the apartment before, but now, sitting on the floor and hugging Jimmy, I wondered. It was an old building. For years and years different people had kept their clothes in this closet and slept in this room. Someone had hated this place. Had that person lived somewhere wonderful once? Like me?

I put the music box back on the windowsill, shut off the light, and crawled back into bed. Now I had something new to keep me awake. Who else, in the middle of the night, had been homesick and lonely in this room? Who else had wanted to leave?

# Chapter Two

The next morning Mom went to work cleaning an apartment on the top floor, leaving me dawdling over breakfast. The doorbell surprised me when I was halfway through my second glass of orange juice. I found Lottie standing in the hall, smiling tentatively.

"How about going for a walk?" she asked. "I'll show you around the neighborhood. You know, all the tourist attractions, like the three-legged dog, and house with the fence made out of soup cans, and the funny-smelling store at the end of the boulevard where you can have your ears pierced or get a tattoo. They've got samples in the window."

"What?" I cried, struggling to hold back my scandalized laughter.

"I'm only kidding, Maryanne. I'll take you to the park, and the schoolyard, and up and down the nice end of the boulevard so you can see what the stores are like."

I didn't know much about the neighborhood. I'd spent nearly all my first days inside the apartment, helping Mom try to fit our belongings into the cramped closets and cupboards. I'd watched a lot of television, too, soap operas and movies. I'd have phoned my old friends, but the calls would have been long-distance, and we couldn't afford that. A walk around the neighborhood sounded good.

"I'll have to tell Mom where I'm going," I said. "She's cleaning a vacant apartment on the top floor this morning."

"The Johnsons' place, I bet," Lottie said. "It'll take her all day because the Johnsons were such pigs."

Mom thought the walk was a good idea, so a few minutes later, Lottie and I left. When we reached the sidewalk, I heard paper rattling in the light wind and looked up to see a long strip of shelf liner hanging from one of the balconies. On it, someone had writ-ten: "TOM, get a haircut. TODAY."

I began laughing, but Lottie said, "Isn't that mean? Tom's mother does that. The signs drive Mrs. Eldrich crazy, because nobody's supposed to put anything out-side where people driving by might notice it. She acts as if there are thousands of cars lined up waiting to see the Two Arms, when the real truth is people probably go out of their way to avoid looking at us. But Tom's mother does exactly as she pleases, so there's a different sign practically every week."

"How long have the Kingsleys lived here?" I asked as we crossed the street to walk in the shade of a line of old birch trees.

"They've been here a year or two longer than Mom and me," Lottie said. "They used to live in Portland. Tom's friend, Vic—he lives in the Other Arm— moved in about the same time and they've been best friends ever since."

We walked several blocks to the boulevard, passing from our own shabby neighborhood to a nicer one where the houses and yards had been cared for. Lottie was oblivious to the neat lawns and flower beds, but I caught myself smiling at the sights. Once I bent and pulled a weed from the edge of a driveway.

At my house—the house where we'd lived when Dad was alive—the roses would be wonderful now. Were the new owners taking care of them? This had been a bad year for insects.

We turned the corner to the boulevard, and Lottie said, "This is the espresso shop where Mom works."

I glanced through the windows. "Nice," I said, re-membering now that Lottie's mom had two jobs. That sounded hard. Mom wanted to find a bookkeeping job, but she hadn't had any luck so far.

"Where did you live before you came here?" Lottie asked.

I told her I'd lived in a suburb outside Seattle, but I didn't offer any details. The conversation was heading toward things I didn't really want to talk about. I tried to think of a way to change the subject, but my mind was a blank.

"Is your dad still there?" Lottie asked.

There it was. The question I hated most of all.

"My dad died more than a year ago," I said.

"Oh, I'm sorry!" Lottie cried. "I shouldn't have asked that!"

I tried to shrug but ended up shivering instead. "He had a heart attack," I said, answering the question I knew she wanted to ask next.

"That's awful," Lottie said. "I'm really sorry, Maryanne."

We walked in silence for a few steps, and then Lottie said, "My parents got a divorce two years ago. That's when we moved here. Hey, there's the bookstore, Maryanne. And the ice cream shop. See?"

"Do you know who lived in our apartment before Mom and I moved in?" I asked as I glanced across the street at the stores.

"An old couple from Montana," Lottie said promptly. "The Freelands. They moved to Los Angeles to be close to their daughter."

We waited at the intersection for the traffic light to change. Two boys on bikes careened past and hooted at us. Lottie hooted back.

I barely noticed. I was remembering the writing in the closet, and I didn't think an old person would have done it. "Can you remember who was in the apartment before the Freelands?" I asked.

Lottie pursed her lips. "Let me think. Gee, no, I don't remember. How come you want to know?"

I shrugged. "I was just curious. It seems funny to be living in a place where so many other people have lived."

"I hated the apartment house at first," Lottie said. "But now I'm used to it—except for Martie and her mother, that is. And Monica. Living at the Arms is a little like living in a small town. At least we're never completely alone."

We took the long way home past the small park. I thought it was amazing that Lottie actually liked living in an apartment. How was it possible? No one had much privacy. Everyone could hear people quarreling through the walls and smell their cooking in the halls. And there was no yard, no place to go and sit on a sunny day. No place to plant roses. No view.

On Sunday morning, Mom and I started out early looking for inexpensive furniture. We found a nice oak coffee table at a flea market, two small pine dressers in a yard sale, and a slightly ragged armchair through the classified section of the morning paper. We arrived home in the van just as Tom strolled up.

"Greetings, Russell. Need a hand with your stuff?" he asked. "I'll work for free today."

"Don't call me by my last name," I said crossly.

"Do you need help or not?" He leaned against the

van, making himself comfortable. He'd had his hair cut, I saw, so his mother's efforts had succeeded.

"We could use your strong back getting our things into the elevator," Mom said.

Tom made himself useful, reaching for the coffee table immediately. He was even more useful when a thin girl with frizzy hair shouted at us to take the coffee table back to the service elevator.

"Buzz off, Martie," Tom said. He brushed a little dust off the table and sat on it.

"My mom says . . . " Martie began. Her face was red.

Tom, with an elaborate gesture, reached up to poke the button on the control panel for my floor. "Ta-da," he said. He stood up and bowed to Martie while the elevator doors slid shut.

"Was that Mrs. Eldrich's daughter?" I asked.

"The very one," Tom said. He plopped back down on the coffee table. "Stay away from her, Russell. She's a sneak and a liar and a tattletale. Trust me on this. We're talking industrial-strength bad news here."

I believed him, but I didn't say anything. I wasn't ready to choose up sides yet.

A few minutes later, while we were pulling one of the dressers out of the elevator on the fourth floor, an elderly woman popped out of the apartment across the hall. She looked fragile and grandmotherly, with white hair that was almost transparent, but she wore a dress with red and yellow flowers, and dangling bead earrings. I liked her even before she spoke.

"Here you are, Tom," she said. She smiled vaguely at me.

"Felicitations, Mrs. Thrasher," Tom said.

"Vic went to the store for me two hours ago," Mrs. Thrasher said. "But he isn't back yet. Either something's happened to him or he's been arrested, which he no doubt deserves."

Tom's mouth tightened. "I saw him playing around in the parking lot. I'll find him for you as soon as we get this dresser in Maryanne's room."

"If he hasn't made it to the store yet," Mrs. Thrasher said, "please do something dreadful to him. Something painful, if it's not too much trouble and doesn't make a mess."

"Consider it done," Tom assured her. "Pain, blood, and maybe even some screaming." Mrs. Thrasher went back inside her apartment and slammed the door.

Tom and I picked up the dresser again and staggered down the hall. "Isn't Vic supposed to be your friend?"

"He is. But he's also a nitwit, and he never learns that Mrs. Thrasher has a short temper when somebody lets her down. Now I'll have to chase after him."

Tom practically tossed the dresser into my bedroom and took off running.

"Thanks," I called out to him, but he didn't look back.

I went out to help Mom with the other dresser and explained about Tom. It was hard work getting the dresser as far as the elevator, and most of the time Martie watched us, scowling.

"You aren't supposed to use this elevator to move furniture," Martie told Mom.

"It's too far to the service elevator," Mom barked. "We'd end up carrying it twice as far." I was surprised. Usually Mom didn't sound that sharp, even when she had reason to be angry.

"I'll tell my mother," Martie said.

"Who cares, Martie?" Mom said. "Who cares?" She gave the dresser one last ferocious shove, pushed it into the elevator, and punched the floor button.

"She's not much fun," I observed, snickering a little.

"Tell me about it," Mom said bitterly. "But she's the boss's daughter, or so she reminds me a dozen times a day."

The elevator stopped and we shoved the dresser out into the hall.

"You can find a better job," I said. "One without Martie and her mother."

"You bet," Mom said. "I'll concentrate on it on my next day off. Right now I've got furniture on my mind."

The armchair was still in the van, and that posed a problem because it was much heavier than it looked. I ran to Lottie's apartment and asked if she'd help. The three of us dragged the armchair out of the van— while many people hung over their balconies to watch the struggle. One little girl kept shouting, "That's

Gammie's chair! Those people got Gammie's chair!" I longed to yell back that Gammie was welcome to it because I'd developed a strong hatred for the ugly thing. It was bad enough owning tattered furniture. It was even worse when all your neighbors knew about it—and one thought she recognized it.

"What other stuff are you moving in today?" Lottie asked Mom.

"This is the last of it," Mom said. "My back is killing me! I'm not sure I'll ever be able to straighten up again. Listen, girls, will we get this chair in the elevator without scraping it on the lobby carpet? Wrecking carpet won't make me very popular with you-know-who, and the chair doesn't seem to have any convenient handholds."

Monica Kingsley appeared out of the stairwell, her mouth stained purple and a soiled bandage on her forehead. "You have to pay two dollars to use the elevator on Sundays," she said.

"No, we don't!" Lottie shouted.

"Then I'll help you move that chair for a dollar."

"You're too little," Mom said. "But we could use some grown-up help. Is your dad home?"

"He's gone out," Monica said. "He always goes out on Sundays. I'll go find Mom and my sister."

Mom shouted "No!" at her, but she ran off anyway. We dragged the armchair halfway to the elevator, not expecting Monica to come back, but she did, with her mother and a sister who looked about four years old.

24

"Monica, watch Audrey," Mrs. Kingsley said.

"Do I have to?" Monica whined. "Do I? Do I?"

I could see where Tom and Monica got their blond hair. Mrs. Kingsley had wonderful pale curls pulled back in a ponytail. But the little girl, Audrey, was dark. She sat down on the floor to watch. Without warning, Monica socked her arm, saying, "That's for nothing so don't do something." Audrey scowled and stuck out her tongue.

Mrs. Kingsley told Mom there was a handtruck in the basement for the tenants to use, even though Mrs. Eldrich did her best to keep it a secret. When she brought it up, she and Mom loaded the armchair on it and trundled it into the elevator.

"It's simple when you've got the right tools," Mrs. Kingsley said. "You've been breaking your back for nothing, just the way Eldrich wants you to do. Monica, leave your sister alone. Monica, do you hear me?" She grabbed Monica's arm.

"How many children do you have?" Mom asked Mrs. Kingsley.

"More than I bargained for," she said with a sigh as the elevator rose. "Three I gave birth to and one I married."

I saw that Lottie was struggling to keep from laughing, but Mom looked as if she'd just gotten more of an answer than she wanted.

Once the armchair was in place, Lottie went home. Mrs. Kingsley herded her daughters into the hall and waved good-bye to us. "Come and have coffee some evening," she said to Mom while she aimed a slap at Monica's arm. Monica had just pinched Audrey, who was starting to cry.

When the door closed behind them, I sat on the love seat and Mom sat in the armchair. "Aristocrat Arms, we're home," she said.

Somewhere in the building, a stereo blared country music. I could hear a baby crying frantically. Water ran in the plumbing, and then an awful knocking started up in the pipes.

This isn't home, I thought. But I kept silent. The day had worn me out.

There were too many people in the building. Too much noise. Maybe Lottie liked it that way, but I knew I'd never get used to it.

That night before I went to bed, I put my clothes away in the dresser and set Dad's picture on top of it, along with the unicorn music box and my collection of glass cat figurines.

"I think we're all set," I told Jimmy, who watched everything with interest from his place on the foot of my bed. "More or less, anyway."

I turned out the light and opened the curtains. I couldn't see anything but the lights in the building across the street, not even the moon or stars. Nothing but other people's windows.

No, we're not all set, I thought. A person has to

have something to look at, growing things, trees and grass and flowers, especially things the person grew herself. A person can't just live in a tan box, looking out at another tan box.

If the person doesn't have something to look at and watch, I thought, then she looks inside, where all the worries are. Worries like what will we do if Mom can't find a better job? What will we do if we use up the last of our savings and don't have enough money for clothes and doctors and the dentist? What if the van breaks down again the way it did last winter?

A person *needs* a view.

I picked up the music box and wound it. While it played, the unicorn turned slowly inside a circle of painted flowers.

Do you know where we are, Dad? I thought as I watched the unicorn. Can you see this place?

Oh, Dad, why did everything have to change?

# Chapter Three

On the first day of school, Mom came along to register me. We said good-bye in the hall outside the office, and I walked to my first class, my sneakers whispering along the hall floor. I didn't know many people in that block-long school. Suddenly I wanted to take off running—but I didn't know where to go.

I found Lottie in math class when I got there, and after that I didn't feel so lonely and hollow. But still, being in a strange school was hard. I missed my old friends. My old life. And a persistent worry had nagged at me since the night before, even though it was so stupid it embarrassed me. Where would I sit at lunch? Would Lottie invite me to sit with her and her friends? I had a hunch she knew practically everybody. Or would I end up alone in a corner?

The math teacher sent me to a seat in the same row

with Lottie, who grinned as I passed her. Maybe we'd have other classes together. I crossed my fingers.

As it turned out, when we compared schedules after math we found we had four classes together, including choir.

I worried about where I'd sit at lunch until the end of third period, when I had Lottie to myself for a moment and finally got up enough nerve to ask if I could share a table with her and her friends.

"Where else?" Lottie asked. "We'll probably sit with a few kids from my old grade school, but there'll be room for you."

Another hurdle was behind me. The knot in my stomach relaxed a little.

The day passed almost too quickly. I was certain I'd never remember anything my teachers said, and I knew I'd never be able to find my way back to my locker. Too much had been happening all at once, I thought as I walked into my last class.

"Greetings, Russell," Tom said. "You must not be as dumb as I thought you were. Or else you've wandered in the wrong room."

"Quit calling me by my last name." I slid into the seat behind him. "And what do you mean about the wrong room?"

"This is the advanced placement English class, for teacher's pets and kids who have more than two brain cells," he told me.

"Then why are *you* here?" I scoffed as I made myself

comfortable. "Kids always get told if they're put in advanced classes."

Tom rolled up his eyes. "Not here," he said. "They don't want us to find out we're smarter than the teachers."

"Well, *you're* not, that's for sure," I said.

"Hey, don't come whining to me when you find out you have to do twice as much homework in this class and need help."

"In your dreams," I said.

Tom turned his back, leaving me seething. Fat chance, I thought, that I'd ever go whining to him about anything. When the class was over, I pretended I didn't see him and hurried out the door. Luck was with me. I saw I was only a few feet away from my locker, and I was so relieved I practically cheered.

After school, Lottie and I discussed the classes and the lunch break while we walked home. The school itself wasn't too bad, and the classes had possibilities.

But the cafeteria, we agreed, would probably shorten our lives. There was no kitchen at the school and the food was delivered in individual servings, covered with plastic wrap or clinging damply to the bottoms of disposable containers.

"It looked *used*," I grumbled. "I was afraid I'd find teeth marks in mine."

"I make better stuff than we had today," Lottie said. "I've been fixing my own lunches since fourth grade."

I had already known that after the first day I'd have

to bring lunch from home most of the time to save money. The food I'd tossed in the trash can at noon convinced me it was a good idea.

Lottie and I liked singing in the choir best of all. "And the greatest part of that class today," Lottie said, "was when the choir director sent Tom out of the room for talking so much. He gets worse as the year goes along. Just wait."

"But he says he gets good grades," I said. "He brags about it."

"Sure," Lottie said. "He's some sort of genius, I guess. He's lots smarter than anybody else. But isn't he a pain?"

"The worst," I said.

That night I went through a box of odds and ends I'd shoved into the back of my closet, looking for extra pencils and ballpoint pens. At the bottom of the box I found a folded poster, an old one I'd saved because I liked the picture. I smoothed it out and taped it to the wall beside my window.

Now I've got a view of trees and a lake, I thought, smiling. Nice. But Jimmy watched me skeptically.

"Hey," I said to him. "It's almost as good as the real thing." I wound up my unicorn music box and put it on the bed beside us.

"It wasn't such a bad day," I told him. "I have kids to eat lunch with, and I even found my locker all by myself."

One day Martie told Lottie and me that she and her mother probably would move into a condo before much longer.

"Is your mother going to be manager there, too?" I asked. I hadn't meant to insult Martie, since I was still working hard to get along with everybody—and Martie was more than just a little bit scary—but she took it the wrong way. I suspected she liked misunderstanding people so that she had an excuse to lose her temper.

"You think my mom *has* to work, don't you?" Martie said. Her face turned blotchy. "Well, let me tell you something, she doesn't. She's not broke like your mother. She's just manager at the Aristocrat to make sure things get done right."

"Sure," Lottie said, and she laughed rudely, which really made Martie angry. She didn't say another word, but stomped off, her frizzy hair bouncing on her shoulders.

"I love these people who don't have to work but only do it for fun," Lottie said. "I only do our laundry and clean the bathroom for fun, too."

I was sure that since Martie hated Lottie, she also hated me. That wouldn't have bothered me at my old school, since I'd had lots of friends to choose from there. But I was practically a stranger here, and I didn't want to make waves. I had a long way to go before I could feel as if I belonged, and maybe that day would never come.

Mom couldn't see the problem. "Martie probably wouldn't have liked you anyway, because you're new," she told me over dinner one night. "She wants to upset you when you're the most vulnerable, and I hope you do your best to disappoint her. See if you can make a game out of it."

I helped myself to another spoonful of Mom's bean-and-rice casserole. "Is that how you deal with Mrs. Eldrich?"

Mom groaned and made a face. "Oh, her. I'm trying, but she's had more practice being a monster than I've had trying to put up with one. You know what she told me today? She told me my back wouldn't hurt so much if I lost weight! Well, maybe I could stand to lose a few pounds, but what's killing my back is cleaning the same oven over and over a dozen times because she imagines she sees a speck of grease somewhere in it. But she's still not as hard on me as she is on Margaret Hale. I've seen her hang around the office for half an hour waiting for poor Margaret, so she can tell her she hates her new haircut or her shoes are funny-looking."

"Mrs. Hale should give it right back to her," I said.

"Margaret loves her other job, the one in the espresso shop over on the boulevard," my mother said as she buttered a piece of bread. "Business is so good they're going to hire another waitress part-time. I thought I might apply. We're a bit low on funds and a second job will help."

We aren't just a bit low on funds, I thought, my food turning bitter in my mouth. We are *poor*. I thought of the girls at school who barely acknowledged my existence, the girls with wonderful clothes who probably hung out at the malls together, who had the same ballet teacher. The girls like my friends at my old school.

"I'm sure I can learn to be a good waitress," Mom said. "But I won't earn enough part-time to give up slaving for Mrs. Eldrich."

I scraped the last of the casserole onto my plate. "I could earn money. I could baby-sit and stuff like that."

Mom made a sound, a sort of humming noise. She did that when she was thinking things over but wasn't in the mood for an argument. Finally she said, "Has anybody asked you to baby-sit?"

"Mrs. Kingsley wants me to watch the girls on Saturday mornings so she can go shopping in peace," I said. "Actually, she said she wanted Lottie and me to baby-sit together. So I told her I'd think about it."

"What about horrible Monica?" Mom asked. "Can the two of you handle her?"

"Mrs. Kingsley said she'd only stay away an hour the first time, just in case. Then we'll see how it goes."

Mom nodded. "Sounds reasonable. I think you can try it."

"And Mrs. Thrasher needs somebody to carry her groceries home," I said. "Lottie and I can take turns helping her. Mrs. Thrasher likes girls to help her more than boys. She says boys drop things or forget them or lose stuff on the way."

Mom drank the last of her coffee. "Okay, I think helping her is a great idea. And that's enough of a career right now, so let's get back to Martie. Can't you just tune her out? We might be here a long time, so you'll have to learn to handle her."

I thought it wouldn't be easy, especially since Martie got such fun out of telling everybody that Mom was her mother's maid, even though that wasn't exactly true. But I didn't want to tell Mom that part of the problem.

"I'll try to go deaf," I said. Privately, I thought I'd like to pull out all Martie's frizzy hair if there was a chance I could get away with it. That was more Lottie's style, and the idea made me smile.

The apartment had a sliding glass door leading to the balcony, but we never left it open, not even when the weather was still hot, because we were afraid Jimmy would fall off the railing. But sometimes I went out by myself and looked up and down the street and wondered how long we'd be there. Maybe only until next summer? Is that what Mom meant by "a long time"? Summer was a million years away.

I could hear several TVs playing in the building,

and someone's radio was turned up so loud that a man was yelling, "Turn it down or I'll bust it. You hear me? You hear me?" Two women were arguing in the apartment below, their voices shrill. "I told you and told you, but you never listen," one cried. "You're stupid, that's why I don't listen," the other responded. I did my best to ignore everything, but I'd need practice.

There wasn't much to see from the balcony. Nothing interesting ever happened on the street, unless the younger children were outside playing sidewalk games. The Executive Arms, opposite us, was made up mostly of one-bedroom apartments occupied by elderly people, so nothing happened there at all. Their windowsill house plants weren't much of a view, either. Most seemed to be dying, probably from lack of light. Our building shaded them all day. And our windows faced north, so we'd have a hard time growing things, too.

I missed having a yard, more than I had ever suspected I could. I'd loved helping Dad in the garden. I liked watching things grow. A garden made the sort of view some people could have and some could not. Once again, money seemed to be the key.

I went inside and turned on the TV. I was sick of thinking about money.

One Saturday afternoon when I was coming home from the library, I saw Tom leaning over the railing of his third-floor balcony, looking up at the sky. I followed his gaze and saw seagulls shifting and sliding on the wind, their white wings shining against the bright blue sky.

Pretty, I thought. Tom must like birds.

Inside the building, a vacuum cleaner was running somewhere, and the halls smelled of garlic. I tried to pretend I liked garlic, but gave up and held my nose.

Mrs. Thrasher phoned me five minutes later, asking if I'd run to the store for her, so I put down my book, gave Jimmy a quick kiss, and took off again. In an hour I was back, with money in my pocket and a handful of Mrs. Thrasher's great oatmeal cookies. I added the money to my secret store in the back of my closet. I was already saving up for Mom's Christmas present. Thanks to Mrs. Thrasher and Mrs. Kingsley, I felt rich. And there was another benefit. If I kept busy, I didn't miss my old friends so much and wonder what they were doing and where they were going without me.

In the last week of September, Mom came home and told me she'd been hired to work at the espresso shop.

"That's great," I said.

"It's exciting, starting something new. Maybe it will turn into a full-time job, and then I can quit working for Mrs. Eldrich. Now let's see, what's for dinner? Don't we have chicken in the freezer?"

Don't get your hopes up yet, I told myself. It would be wonderful if Mom didn't work for Mrs. Eldrich.

Maybe Lottie's mother could quit working for her, too.

Then what would Martie have to talk about at school?

On the first evening Mom worked at the espresso shop, Lottie and I went there to watch. I worried a little about how Mom would feel, having an audience. But when she saw us come in, she smiled and waved.

Lottie's mom sat us at a table in one corner, but she let my mom wait on us. I wanted to try something called a one-shot, but Mom told me all that caffeine would stunt my growth, so I had a decaf latte instead. Lottie knew more about the menu and ordered an exotic decaf espresso drink that involved lots of cream, almonds, and shaved chocolate.

Mom hurried off, looking as if she already knew exactly how to do everything, but an old man with lots of curly white hair and a red scarf around his neck helped her a little with the big espresso machine. When she came back with our cups, the old man came with her.

"This is Mr. Penn," Mom told me. "He owns the shop. Isn't it wonderful?"

I nodded and said, "It sure is." I meant it. It was small, but the tables and chairs were made of beautiful wood, and the walls were mirrored, reflecting the street outside.

Mr. Penn seemed pleased that I was pleased. "Your mama is going to work out fine," he said. "I can tell. She smiles at everybody, even the idiots, and that's good business."

I struggled to keep from laughing. He called some of his customers idiots?

"It's good business," he repeated, and he winked at me.

I did laugh then, and he laughed with me. "Enjoy your latte," he told me. "And come back again. I insist."

He certainly was different from Mrs. Eldrich. She never said much to me except "Don't hang around in the halls, Mary *Jane*." No matter how many times I corrected her, she never remembered.

We stayed for an hour, watching Mom and Mrs. Hale wait on customers, and then, before I was done worrying, Mom told me I had to go because it was getting late.

I wanted to stay a little longer, but Mom darted away to help a couple choose a dessert, so I waved and followed Lottie out the door.

"What do you think?" Lottie asked. "It's a nice place, isn't it? Mr. Penn wants to sell it and retire, so Mom is hoping the new owner will keep her on."

Mom might be a good waitress, but what if the new owner didn't want to keep her? There was no real safety in having a job, or even in owning a store like my father's. Bad things could happen at anytime—really bad things—and people were left with nothing.

I didn't say much on the way home. Mom would be there in another hour and a half, so maybe I'd ask her then if she thought she'd have a job after Mr. Penn sold the place. Then again, maybe asking her wouldn't be such a smart idea. There was no point in bringing up bad news after her first day.

Jimmy was glad to see me when I let myself into the apartment. I carried him into my bedroom and started my homework. I'll keep busy, I told myself, and not think about Mom possibly losing her job.

But the past caught up with me. One loss had followed another, until the last awful day when we had driven away from the house without looking back.

I pushed the homework away, took Jimmy back to the living room, and switched on the television. There was nothing on that appealed to me, so I switched it off again and picked up one of Mom's magazines.

Inside I found a picture of a country house surrounded by a landscaped yard. In the distance, a long line of oak trees stretched to a lake.

I'll have a house like that someday, I thought. I cut that picture out along with several from the other magazines, and put them in the shoe box I used for the snapshots of my old house. I kept my collection hidden in my closet.

Sometimes I crouched down and looked at the secret writing on my closet wall and wondered about the person who had put it there. How had everything turned out for that person?

Had things gotten even worse?

# Chapter Four

"I like walking back and forth to school, even in the rain," I told Lottie one afternoon while we shared an umbrella on the way home. "I rode the bus at my old school, and it was like a zoo on wheels. If we ever go back to our old neighborhood, I hope we have a place closer to school so I can walk."

"I bet you miss your friends," Lottie said. She was coughing and fishing through her pockets, looking for a tissue. "I was sure lonely when I first came here."

Before I could answer, Tom caught up with us and fell into step. His baseball cap and jacket were soaked, but he didn't seem to care.

"What ho, Russell," he said. "You, too, Lottie. Ahoy and all that other good stuff."

I had given up trying to stop him from calling me by my last name. "Where's your pal from the Other

Arm?" I asked. We almost never saw him without Vic.

"Vic's got detention," Tom said.

"How come you don't?" I asked.

"All my teachers are crazy about me," Tom said. "They never send me to detention."

"Yeah, yeah," I grumbled as I scuffed through the wet leaves on the sidewalk.

"What did Vic do that was so awful?" Lottie asked.

"He forgot to show up for detention last Wednesday."

"Vic's an idiot," I said. I wanted to laugh, but they were both truly annoying in class and probably deserved the detention they got. "You two are always playing around, making the teachers mad. Why can't you grow up?"

"Is this what we're going to talk about all the way home, Russell?" Tom complained. "Don't you ever do anything but nag?"

I gave this some thought, and decided he might have a point. "But some people just ask for it," I said finally.

"How do you two like baby-sitting my sisters on Saturdays?"

"They're cute most of the time," Lottie said.

"You mean Audrey's cute," I said. "Monica is a major pain."

"We're planning to lock her in the bathroom," Lottie said. "Listen, Tom, I'm sorry you lost your job for Mrs. Thrasher. But Vic made her so mad, fooling around and always being late."

"It's his fault, not yours," Tom said. "But I still like Mrs. Thrasher. She's a neat old lady, once you get used to her."

"How come she lives in our building instead of across the street at the Other Arm where there aren't any little kids?" I asked. "You'd think she'd get sick of all the noise."

"She likes kids," Tom said. "Except for Monica, but nobody likes her. The manager wants Mrs. Thrasher to move so her apartment can be rented out for lots more money. Mrs. T's got this long cheap lease, see, but she's staying until she gets a place in a retirement village with her friends."

I stared at him and nearly tripped over a curb. "How do you know all that? It sounds like you eavesdrop on people."

"Sure. Don't you? You can hear everything in the Arms."

I couldn't imagine a time when I'd care enough about what was happening to anybody in that place to pay attention to what I overheard.

Then suddenly it occurred to me that if I could hear the other tenants, they could hear me. Wonderful.

"I'll never get used to living in an apartment," I said.

We were half a block from home and I could already see a long strip of wet paper flapping on Tom's balcony. Tom was in trouble again, but he didn't know it yet.

"Hey, this isn't a bad place, Russell," Tom said. "I've lived here a million years and I'm only a little bit crazy."

Lottie had looked up and seen the sign, and now she hurried a little faster, almost as if she wanted Tom to pass under the sign without noticing it. But Tom finally saw it dangling from his balcony, so he stepped into the street to get a better view of his mother's message.

"'The maid quit, Tom. Clean your bedroom,'" he read aloud.

I laughed. "I love your mom's notes."

"Yeah?" he said angrily. "Well, I don't." He ran ahead of us and disappeared inside the building without even saying good-bye.

"I guess Tom doesn't think his mother's very funny," I said.

"Neither do I," Lottie said between bouts of coughing. "Gee, I'm starting to feel really awful. I'm going to lie down for a while. Can we do our homework later on?"

"Take care of yourself," I said. "Call me if you need anything. Promise?"

Since Dad had died, I worried about people when they got sick.

☙

Both Mrs. Hale and Mom worked at the espresso shop most evenings, so Lottie and I spent lots of time together, doing homework or watching TV. Actually, I watched more TV than Lottie, because she spent her free time sewing. She made most of her own clothes.

But on the day she came down with her awful cold, she had barely started on her homework by the time I knocked on her door carrying my load of books and papers.

Lottie let me in and then crawled back into the bed she had made for herself on the couch. "This isn't the worst cold I've ever had," she said. She blew her nose hard. "But I'm on my second box of tissues, and I'm starting to hate television." She blew her nose again, and then began laughing. "Guess what? Martie came by a while ago to tell me she's best friends with Dolly Malone now and Dolly isn't going to sit with us in the cafeteria anymore."

"What?" I cried. "Martie said that? Dolly hates her. Last week she dumped her whole carton of yucky tapioca pudding on Martie's lunch when Martie said her hair looked like something exploded in it."

"Martie's jealous," Lottie said. "Before I moved here, she and Tom and Vic used to walk to school together. I think she's got a crush on Vic. But after I came, they started walking with me, and Martie's been mad ever since."

"Well, being so mean won't win her any friends back," I said. "Here, I brought us chocolate cupcakes. Have you done your math yet?" I sat down on the floor next to the couch and got out my math paper.

"Oh, sure, I finished math and while I was at it, I

got ready for the science quiz on Friday, too," Lottie said grumpily as she dug through her bathrobe pockets until she found more tissue. She blew her nose so hard her eyes watered. "Maryanne, if you can actually work all those problems, go home and gloat. I'm too sick to watch you."

"I only did half of them," I said. "I don't even understand the questions."

"I know who never has trouble with math," Lottie said. "Tom. We could ask him for help."

"Are you kidding?" I cried. "I'd rather die."

"He gets all As," Lottie said. "Let's call him."

"Over my dead body," I said. "I mean it. He's the last person I want to help me."

"Hey, let's ask Martie if she's worked all the problems," Lottie said. Her laugh sounded more like a croak.

"In her dreams," I grumbled.

Get help from Martie? I thought. That'll be the day. I turned pages in my math book, hoping for a miracle. Once I'd been good at math—at everything in school. I still managed fairly well in most things, but math—I was beginning to think my brain had dried up. I couldn't concentrate anymore.

"I don't know why things have to change," I said.

Lottie stared at me. "What are you talking about?"

I shrugged, embarrassed. "I don't know. Nothing, I guess. But I was remembering I used to be good at math. It makes me mad that Tom is and I'm not."

"You had a really bad year," Lottie said.

I cleared my throat hard. "So? Did I have to turn stupid?"

We sat in silence for a moment, and then Lottie blurted, "I wouldn't feel nearly as bad if my dad had died. But he ran away from us. From me, I guess." She looked down, plucking at the stitches in her quilted bathrobe.

"He didn't run away from you," I said.

"How do you know?" Lottie demanded.

I spread my hands helplessly. "I don't. But you're nice, Lottie. Why would he leave because of you?"

Lottie shrugged. "I don't know. He just did, that's all."

"Is that what your mother says?" I asked, horrified.

Lottie shook her head. "Of course not. She says it wasn't my fault."

"Then whose fault was it?" I asked.

Big tears splashed on Lottie's math book. "It doesn't matter, because he got married again right afterward," she said. "Her name is Laura. I guess he liked her better than he did us."

I tried to imagine how I would have felt if Dad had left Mom and me instead of dying. That would have been terrible, but I'd rather have had him alive, even if I was angry and hurt. At least I could see him sometimes. At least I wouldn't have those awful split-second lapses when I forgot he was dead and thought he was lost someplace and couldn't find us.

"Let's not talk about depressing stuff anymore," I said.

"Good idea," Lottie said, and she wiped her eyes on another tissue. "Did you know that Mrs. Eldrich told Tom's mother that if bratty Monica doesn't stay out of the elevator, the whole family will be evicted?"

I grinned. "What did Mrs. Kingsley say?" Tom's mother always had a sharp answer for everything.

"She told Mrs. Eldrich to quit creeping around in the halls spying on people," Lottie said. "She said, 'Get a life, even if you have to borrow one!'"

"Mrs. Eldrich took it out on Mrs. Thrasher," I said. "When I was going through the lobby, I heard Mrs. Thrasher ask her if she could please have her oven repaired, and Mrs. Eldrich said, 'Eventually,' so then Mrs. Thrasher said, 'In this century?' and Mrs. Eldrich got really snotty and said, 'Don't be ridiculous. Are you done? Because I have more important things to do than talk to you. And stop hanging around the lobby.'"

"She didn't!" Lottie cried. "Mrs. Thrasher is so nice!"

"Mrs. Eldrich has been grouchy all week," I said. "She made Mom go back to the Other Arm twice to clean a kitchen because she said she didn't do a good enough job."

"Doesn't your mom hate her?" Lottie asked. "Mine does. We have this big joke between us. Every time we hear a loud noise in the hall, I say, 'Did Eldrich fall down the stairwell?' and Mom says, 'Oh, be still my heart. If only it could be true.'"

I laughed for a long time and then said, "Mom needs the job, at least for a while. But some day she'll quit."

I got a knot in my stomach every time I remembered how much Mom did need the job. She kept saying things would get better at the espresso shop, she'd get more hours like Mrs. Hale, and pretty soon that might be her only job. But the sandwich shop half a block away had gone out of business the first week in October. What had happened to the people who worked there?

The weather got cold the following week, and the rain that fell turned to snow. One morning Lottie and I walked to school on sidewalks glittering with frost, past houses with windows decorated for Halloween.

"Are you excited about the Halloween dance?" Lottie asked. She was so cold her nose was red, and she rubbed it with a mittened hand.

"I'm not going," I said. "Why would I go to a dance?"

"You are too going," Lottie said. "It'll be fun. I love after-school dances."

"When all the girls stand on one side of the room and watch all the boys on the other side punch each other and fool around?" I asked. "That's not fun."

"Did the boys in your school do that, too?" Lottie

asked. "How many dances did you have in sixth grade?"

"We had three," I said. "The last one was canceled because the boys all signed a letter saying they wouldn't go."

"That's awful," Lottie said. "Well, we're having a dance once a month, unless the boys here do the same thing. But I think they'll dance. They're older now, and they'll want to."

"You must have gone crazy and I didn't notice until now," I said. "Can you imagine Tom dancing with anybody?"

The idea struck us so funny that we laughed the rest of the way to school. "You'll see," I told her. "The boys won't dance."

And I was right, too. The Halloween dance was a failure from the beginning, because the boys didn't just refuse to dance. Most of them stayed in the drafty hall outside the gym doors, making fun of everybody who went inside. A few of them ran in to grab food off the tables and then ran out to the hall again, to supply their friends.

"See?" I reminded Lottie as we watched Tom making his second trip back through the door with a handful of doughnuts. "Why should they come in here when they're getting everything they want out there?"

"Maybe they would have danced if this had been a costume party," Lottie said.

"They wouldn't have worn costumes, either," I said.

"Let's face it. If we want to dance, we're going to have to dance with each other."

"So what else is new?" Lottie said.

But Lottie didn't seem to mind. One nice thing about her was that she always had a good time. Before the afternoon was over, she'd danced with several girls, and then actually invited scowling Martie out on the floor, too.

"We had as good a time as those girls over there," I told Lottie, cocking my head toward the corner where the in crowd stood.

"In grade school, they were friendlier," Lottie said. "At school, anyway. Now they only hang around with each other."

I remembered clearly how things had been at my old school. The girls with the best clothes and largest allowances made a few school friends among the girls who didn't have as much. But they almost never made after-school friends with those same girls. I ought to know, because I'd been one of the in crowd in my old school. I hadn't wanted to hurt anybody's feelings, but it was easier to do things with the friends you made from your own neighborhood, or the ones who took ballet and music lessons from the same teachers you did. The ones who had money to spend at the malls, instead of hanging around watching the others.

"Your clothes are just as nice as theirs," I said. "Better. You know that, don't you?"

"What difference does it make?" Lottie said. "I

want to be a dress designer someday, so I work really hard on my clothes. But those girls will never invite me to one of their parties."

I grabbed Lottie's arm and turned her back on the in girls. "Who cares? Nobody thinks about them except themselves. And Martie."

"Sure," Lottie said. "But let's go home now, okay?"

"Sounds good to me," I said. "Let's get our jackets."

When we left, Lottie said, "Maybe next time the teachers will choose better music and more of the kids will dance."

I laughed. "You mean more of the girls? The boys still won't."

Lottie grinned and shrugged. "I suppose you're right. Someday they'll be sorry. Someday they'll be dying to dance with us and we'll turn them down."

"You really are crazy," I said.

"Admit it. Wasn't this better than trick-or-treating?" Lottie asked.

"Yes, since it's raining outside," I said. "But I'd rather have dressed up in a costume and gone from door to door inside the building with Monica and Audrey."

"Now who's crazy?" Lottie said. "Monica would mug you in the hall for your candy."

We ran home laughing, ignoring Tom, who ran after us yelling for us to wait. He didn't deserve to have us wait for him. Maybe someday Lottie would be right and Tom would be dying to dance with me. But I wouldn't. No way. I'd leave him standing there, looking like a big jerk, with everybody laughing at him.

I didn't tell that to Lottie, though. She'd wonder why I cared, and I wouldn't have an answer.

# Chapter Five

On the day before Thanksgiving, heavy wet snow began falling unexpectedly in the middle of the morning. By the time school was out, the snow lay deep on the ground, muffling city sounds and disguising the familiar sight of neglected yards.

Lottie had worn boots, but I only had sneakers, so my feet were cold and wet by the time we'd trudged a few blocks toward home. And snow was still falling, blowing sideways in the wind. When I looked up, I was amazed to see two seagulls flapping overhead, barely visible, heading toward Puget Sound a couple of miles away.

"Where do they go in snowstorms?" I asked Lottie. She didn't know either, so I worried about the birds, something I'd never done before.

"I wish we were going home to a big fireplace," I

said, remembering the one in my house. It seemed as if I'd been gone from there for a million years.

"How about a woodstove?" Lottie said. "We had a woodstove when I was little, and on days like this Mom would light a fire and put on a pan of water with cloves and a cinnamon stick floating in it. It smelled like something wonderful was baking in the oven."

I brushed snow off my face. "Instead of the way the Arms smells. Ugh."

"I know," Lottie said. "The place smells horrible. But I'm used to living in an apartment. I like having lots of people around. I like knowing all the neighbors, except the Eldrich witches. Our house was in the middle of a big field, and at night it seemed really creepy."

Privately I thought a house in the middle of a big field sounded great.

The Hales were having Thanksgiving dinner with Mom and me, and Mom had taken the afternoon off so she could shop. By the time I got home, Mom was unpacking most of the foods that made the holiday meal special to us. "The turkey's coming later, with Margaret," Mom said.

"I hope she's not letting it drive," I said soberly. "The streets are a mess."

Mom burst out laughing, the way I'd known she would. "That's not bad for somebody who's soaking wet. You'd better change shoes right away. In fact, change everything. You look as if you're freezing."

"Look who's talking," I said. "Your shoes are wet, too. And you sound as if you're catching a cold."

The snow stopped falling around eleven that night, and I went to bed. Jimmy curled up on my feet, purring.

The next morning we were busy in the kitchen by eight. Lottie and her mother showed up at noon, bringing a salad, rolls, and a plate of applesauce cookies "just to see us through until dinner," Mrs. Hale said.

"The turkey smells wonderful," Lottie said. "Everybody's turkey smells great. I could tell who's home and who isn't on this floor as we passed their doors."

"Has Mrs. Thrasher left yet?" I asked.

"Her friend came earlier and got her," Lottie said. "I saw her in the hall, and she said this will be her last Thanksgiving here—if she's lucky. Her friend thinks there'll be an apartment available in the retirement village pretty soon. Some man named Charlie is moving to California."

"Think of it—palm trees and warm weather instead of snow," I said as I sampled one of the cookies.

"Somehow warm weather doesn't go with turkey," Lottie said. "For once I don't mind snow staying on the ground."

Mrs. Hale took my place in the kitchen, helping Mom. The two mothers got along as well as we did. I heard Mom say, "But do you think we could?"

Mrs. Hale said, "Of course. How can we fail?"

Mom groaned and said, "You believe pigs can fly, too." Both of them laughed.

"I bet they're talking about the shop again," Lottie said. "Mr. Penn's putting it up for sale after the first of the year, and Mom says he's been telling them they ought to buy it."

"You're kidding," I said uneasily. "Mom never mentioned that. An espresso shop must cost an awful lot." I'd been hoping Mom would find a way for us to have a house again, even if we only rented one. I was sure she wouldn't spend what was left of our savings on Mr. Penn's shop.

"Oh, he'll make them a good deal, if they actually go through with it," Lottie said. She was changing channels on the TV set, looking for something other than football.

I didn't want to think about the espresso shop anymore, so I made an excuse to wander into the kitchen.

"There's only room for two people in here," Mrs. Hale said, laughing. "If you come in, I'll have to go out."

"I wanted a glass of water," I said. "How's your cold, Mom?"

"I forgot about it. All I needed was good hot tea and some sleep."

"And plenty of turkey today," Mrs. Hale said.

I drank the water I didn't want and went back to the living room to page restlessly through the *TV Guide*.

"I'm hungry," Lottie said. "I could eat cat food. I could even eat school food."

And at that moment, the lights and television went off.

"Oh no!" Mom and Mrs. Hale yelled at the same time.

"The power's gone out," Lottie said. "I don't believe it. Not on Thanksgiving."

I looked out the windows. I couldn't see a single light burning anywhere. It was a power failure, all right, and not just in our apartment.

"It'll come back on in a minute," I said. "It always does."

But the lights stayed out. After half an hour, Mrs. Hale called the power company, got put on hold for ten minutes, and finally learned that we'd be without power for several hours.

"What are we going to do with that turkey?" Mom asked. "It's only half done."

"Let's stick it in the refrigerator," Mrs. Hale said. "Maybe the man was wrong. Maybe the power will be back on in a few minutes and we can start cooking again. We'll hope for the best."

"I don't want to eat anything that we have to hope for the best about," I said. "That sounds too much like lunch at school." Lottie laughed, and finally I did, too, but I meant what I said.

"I see your point," Mom told me. "We don't need food poisoning. Okay, if the power doesn't come back immediately, then we'll forget the turkey. Anybody have any other suggestions for dinner?"

"Let's ask around the building and see who's got what already cooked," Mrs. Hale said. "Maybe we can combine things. Lots of people will have stuff for salads."

"And rolls and butter and things like that," Mom said.

"And olives and pickles," I added.

"And pumpkin pie," Lottie said.

"We could have a sort of potluck," Mom said. She was beginning to sound as if she liked this idea.

"Let's go out and see what we can find," Mrs. Hale said.

It didn't take long to locate a dozen families who were wondering what they were going to do now that they couldn't cook anything. The Kingsleys suggested that we all leave our doors open and put whatever we had out on tables and let people swap things after everybody had had a chance to look around.

"We'll carry around our own plates," Mrs. Hale said.

"Sounds good," Mom said.

So we pulled on our jackets, because the building was getting cold, equipped ourselves with dinner plates and flashlights, and started on our rounds, up and down the stairs, back and forth in the dark halls, and ended up, after a couple of hours, nearly too full of food to walk. Then I understood how Lottie felt about living there and knowing nearly everyone. It was almost like being in a small town, with everyone sharing a hard time and making the best of it. If Mom and I had been alone in a house somewhere, the day wouldn't have ended up being much fun. Maybe being here wasn't so bad. Maybe.

Tom and Monica came back to our apartment with us because Mrs. Hale had promised them the leftover applesauce cookies. It was dark by then, and their flashlights were getting dim, so Mom set out all the candles she had.

"I don't know how you can eat anything else," Lottie told Tom. "I counted the pieces of pie you put away."

"I counted the helpings you ate of my mom's crab salad," Tom said. "Oink." He took a handful of the cookies, passed half to Monica, and looked around. "Where's your cat, Russell?" he asked me. "You didn't let him get out of the apartment, did you?"

"Certainly not," I said. "I shut him in my bedroom."

"I wanna see your cat," Monica said. She ran down the short hall and opened Mom's bedroom door.

"Hey," Mom said. "Stay out of my room."

"I don't want her in my room, either," I said. I ran after Monica, but I was too late, because she opened my door and ran inside, yelling for Jimmy.

My room was dark and I could barely see Jimmy standing on my pillow with his back arched. Monica made a grab for him, but Jimmy shot away, crawling behind my wobbly old dresser.

"Monica, leave him alone!" I yelled, but Monica never listened to anyone.

Before I could stop her, she grabbed a corner of the dresser and pulled it away from the wall. Jimmy ran out of the room, hissing, and Tom, coming down the hall, nabbed him.

"Got him!" he called out.

At that instant, I heard a crash. When I turned, I saw that the dresser had tipped over. I knew from the sound that my glass cats had broken, and if I could have caught Monica, I might have socked her. I really wanted to.

The lights went on in the living room.

I reached for the bedroom wall switch and turned on the ceiling light. Monica stood there, looking pale and scared. The dresser lay on the floor with glass all around.

In the middle of the mess I saw the music box, with the unicorn broken off and smashed to bits.

It couldn't be broken! It was too awful. But it was, it was!

"Look what you did!" I shouted at Monica. "You broke my music box! That was the last Christmas present my dad gave me and you broke it! Get out of here right now. You get out of here before I—before I . . . "

I ran at Monica, my fists clenched, tears pouring down my face. Monica disappeared, but I couldn't stop crying.

Mom grabbed me and hugged me. "Stop, baby,

stop," she said. "Maryanne, we can find another one."

But I couldn't stop my tears. I didn't even want to try. The music box was my last gift from Dad. There would never be another like it, not ever. *Not ever!*

I pulled loose from Mom and bent down to gather up the music box and the broken bits of the unicorn. Lottie came in and tried to help, but I pushed her away.

"She has to do this herself," Lottie's mother said quietly. "Let her take care of this alone. She'll know best what to do."

Everybody left. I wiped my eyes on my sleeve and picked up the broken pieces by myself. Finally I wound the music box. It still played, but the box was ruined.

I sat for a long time in my room, holding what was left of the music box, watching the unicorn's broken feet turning stupidly on the little gilt stand. And Dad was lost somewhere in the dark on Thanksgiving—on Thanksgiving!—not knowing why we weren't in the house anymore or where we'd gone. Lost.

Oh, Daddy. I don't like it here. I hate this place.

I hate this place.

I jumped up and opened my closet door. There, on the wall near the floor, somebody had written those words. I pawed through my box of school supplies and found a red felt-tipped pen. I shoved back my clothes to make room, knelt on the floor, and printed "I hate this place" on the wall over the other writing. And then I printed it again. And again.

I HATE THIS PLACE.

I HATE THIS PLACE.

I HATE THIS PLACE.

I didn't know I was screaming until Mom came in and grabbed me.

"Maryanne, what's wrong?" she cried. "Oh, honey, what are you doing? Maryanne, please."

I turned and wrapped my arms around her neck, hard. "I don't want to be here anymore," I cried. "Why did he die? It wasn't fair. I can't stay here. I want to go home."

The next morning I got up late. Mom had left a note on the table. "Gone to clean an apartment at the Other Arm," she had written. "Back for lunch. I love you very much."

I ate breakfast and then sat down on the couch with Jimmy on my lap. Through the dining room window I could see water dripping from the balcony above. The snow was melting. A TV somewhere in the building was tuned to a game show. People screamed and clapped. I didn't care about anything.

Someone knocked on the door, and I sat there for a few moments, wondering if I wanted to talk to anybody. Finally I answered.

"I bid you good morning," Tom said. "You okay, Russell?"

"What do you want?" I asked coldly.

His face turned red. For a moment, all he could do was stammer. Finally he said, "I'm really sorry about what my sister did. If it makes you feel any better, she has to stay in her room all day. And my mom said she'd get you another music box."

"I don't want another music box," I said, and I closed the door in his face.

Stupid Monica. Stupid Tom.

I went back to my bedroom and took the shoe box out of my closet. For a long time I sat on the floor with Jimmy, looking at the pictures of houses. I liked some better than others, but any of them would satisfy me. One house had daffodils blooming under a willow. I touched the picture, remembering how good the earth smelled when I dug in it to plant bulbs.

# Chapter Six

Jimmy liked dragging shoes around. Usually he picked Mom's, but sometimes he chose mine instead. He left teeth marks, and only stared haughtily when he was scolded.

"He doesn't have anything to do when we're gone," I told Mom while I tried to rub out the teeth marks in my boots with a rough towel. "He used to have a good view out our windows. Here all he can see is the Other Arm. I think he's bored."

"Maybe we should leave the TV on for him," Mom said. I expected her to laugh, but she looked serious. "I've heard of pets who watch TV."

"He can keep up on the soaps for me," I said as I tugged on one of my boots.

"You can't wear those to school," Mom said. "The soles are worn out. They'll leak."

"My sneakers would leak worse," I said.

"Oh, Lord," Mom said, sighing. "I should have bought you new boots weeks ago."

"I won't get my feet wet—there are lots of clear places on the sidewalk."

"Take my boots," Mom said. "They ought to fit. I'm working here today and I won't need them. We'll get you new ones this evening. I've got money tucked away for emergencies."

I zipped up my jacket while Mom got the boots. She didn't know how much money I'd saved—she never kept track. Probably I had enough to buy my own boots. But then I wouldn't have enough to get her a good Christmas present. I didn't know which to choose. That was one of about a zillion problems that being broke could cause. You had to make awful choices.

There was a faint line between Mom's eyes when she brought back the boots. The worry line decided me.

"I've saved enough for new boots," I said. "Between Mrs. Kingsley and Mrs. Thrasher, I've been making lots of money this last month."

"You shouldn't have to spend it on boots," Mom said. She shook her head. The line between her eyes was a little deeper.

"Look, you provide the ride to the shoe store and I'll provide the money tonight," I said. I grabbed my lunch sack. "Lottie will be waiting by the elevator. I'll see you later."

66

I ran out of the apartment before Mom had a chance to argue. Part of me was pleased—I was acting like a grown-up and taking responsibility. But part of me was in a panic. I hadn't decided what to get Mom for Christmas yet, but I wanted it to be something really special. And really expensive. We'd been scraping along on practically nothing for what seemed like forever.

Well, I'd just have to think of something. Or find more work so I could earn more money. Did other kids worry this much? Was there ever an end to it?

When Lottie and I reached the lobby, we saw Martie coming down the hall from her apartment, but the instant she saw us, she scurried out the front door.

"She could walk with us, I suppose," Lottie said. "If she kept her big mouth shut and quit criticizing everybody, that is. I don't think she has any idea of how to act."

I laughed at that. Martie would be nice if only she knew how. Sure. So would a rattlesnake.

The temperature had dropped during the night, and the half-melted snow had frozen on the sidewalks into lumpy sheets of ice. We slipped and skidded all the way to school—and enjoyed the sight of Martie, hurrying half a block ahead of us, falling on her rear in front of the big yellow house Lottie and I called the Castle.

The house was old, but it had been restored. There was a round tower on one side, rising above the second floor. The front door had a stained-glass panel with bright red roses and green leaves. Every time I passed it, I imagined myself walking through that beautiful door. But to be absolutely perfect, the house should have been out in the country with fields and woods around. There should have been a big garden and lots of flowers.

"Look!" Lottie said, pointing.

There was a Christmas tree standing in the first-floor bay window.

"It's too early for a tree," I said. "It'll be all dried out by Christmas."

"If I lived in that house," Lottie said, "I'd leave the tree up all year round."

We'll have a Christmas tree in the apartment, I thought. It will have to be small. I caught myself smiling in anticipation, and surprised myself.

"I wouldn't eat cafeteria food if I was starving," Lottie said that day during lunch break. "Mom says the people who make the lunches for Maple Street School make meals for airlines, too, and they wouldn't recognize good food if it fell on them."

While she talked, she opened her dark blue nylon lunch bag and started taking things out. She had a banana nut muffin the size of a saucer, a container of strawberry jam, another container filled with sliced vegetables, a bunch of red grapes, a cup of chocolate pudding, and a silver spoon. "Yum," she said.

I had a cheese sandwich, an apple, and two store-bought chocolate-chip cookies. That was worth half a "yum," I thought, envying Lottie. Her lunches were as creative as the clothes she made for herself. I didn't seem to have a talent for anything.

The cafeteria was crowded and noisy, and usually I didn't pay much attention to Tom and his friends, although they made the most racket. But that day Tom walked around a lot, scowling and showing something to people at different tables. When he came to us, several of his friends were following him. Tom's catastrophes were always more interesting than anyone else's.

"Look at this," he said, shoving his sandwich at us. "See that piece of greasy paper between the bread slices? They didn't even *draw* a picture of ham and cheese on it. All I got was paper!"

"Yeah, paper," Vic echoed. "Gross."

"Did you make that sandwich yourself?" Lottie asked, snickering.

"What?" Tom cried. "Are you crazy? No, I paid good money for this. Stale bread and paper!"

I flinched when he shoved the sandwich close to my face. "I see, I see," I said. "Bread and paper. Somebody made a mistake, Tom. Why don't you just ask for something else instead of coming unglued over it?"

"I did!" Tom said. "I said I wanted a real sandwich or my money back, but I didn't get that either."

"Why not?" Lottie asked.

"Mrs. Dodd said *I* put the paper in the sandwich," Tom said.

Mrs. Dodd was one of the servers, and I found it easy to believe that she wouldn't give Tom his money. She was always crabby and defensive about the food.

But I also knew that Tom loved practical jokes. "Tell the truth. Did you put the paper in it?" I asked.

"No!" he said. "Why would I do that? I'm hungry and I spent the last of my money, and now I don't have anything to eat!"

"Why don't you make your own lunch?" I said.

Without replying, Tom stomped away, still holding the sandwich.

"I bet there isn't a boy in this school who knows how to make a lunch," I said. "Tom would ten times rather have something to yell about than spend five minutes in the kitchen before he leaves for school."

But I couldn't convince Tom I was right, and he harped on that sandwich for days.

"There's a principle involved," he told us on the way home from school a few days later. "We've got a right to buy real food, not paper. And I don't care if it was a mistake somebody made. Somebody should have checked to make sure the sandwich was all right. I should get my money back, and an apology, too."

"Dream on," Lottie told him. "You won't get either from Mrs. Dodd."

"She'll be sorry," Tom said. He took off running to catch up with Vic, who was half a block ahead.

"Tom had better be careful," I said. "Lately Mrs. Dodd's been looking as if she's ready to blow up and make a mess all over the cafeteria ceiling."

"He's never careful," Lottie said. "You wouldn't believe the trouble he started in grade school. Every time he gets mad at his family, he makes trouble at school. I bet he's more mad at Monica than he is at the food—because of your unicorn, you know. But if he fights with her, his dad punishes him. Mr. Kingsley's really mean."

"You mean all this happened because Monica broke my music box?" I asked, appalled.

Lottie shrugged. "The whole family is still having a big fight over it. I heard my mom talking to Mrs. Kingsley. Mr. Kingsley likes Monica best and whatever she does is okay with him. He spoils her when he's home, so Monica thinks she doesn't have to mind her mother or anybody else. And they fight a lot—Tom's mom and dad, I mean."

I was horrified. "I can't believe Tom is in trouble because of me. And he tried to apologize to me and I slammed the door in his face. Now I feel awful."

"It's not your fault. And it's dumb for him to come to school and start something here because he's mad at his family," Lottie said. "So in a way, he's asking for a hard time, and he'll end up getting it, too."

On the following day, Tom started another argument with Mrs. Dodd during lunch break, threw his tray of food on the floor in front of her, and stomped out. He got an hour of detention.

"It's not so bad," he told me that evening in the downstairs hall. "There's me and Vic, who's always in detention. And Gary Proko—he stole Mrs. Fisher's umbrella and stuck it in the library book return bin and opened it up and now nobody can get it out. And there's Eldon Ackerman, who hasn't done homework since school started in September and says he's never going to do it. And Dolly Malone."

"Dolly," I said, shocked. "What could she have done?"

"She won't tell me. When I asked her, she twisted my ear until it practically snapped off, and then she told the detention proctor I hit her."

"Dolly?" I asked, amazed.

"We call her Demolition Dolly now," Tom said. "She's great—if you don't get too close." He was grinning as if Dolly was his girlfriend.

The snow melted and warm rains began falling. On Saturday Lottie and I went Christmas shopping with Mrs. Thrasher, so that we could help her with packages. Snow on the downtown streets would have been prettier, but rain was easier to get around in. But the rain was depressing, too. At least, something was depressing me. And I didn't feel that way just because I'd spent most of my money on new boots.

I could remember so many Christmas holidays when I'd gone shopping with both my parents. I could even remember visiting Santa and having my picture taken. When we passed a long line of little kids waiting to talk to Santa, I turned my head away.

And looked straight at Lottie, who had tears in her eyes.

Both of us blinked and looked past each other. I didn't need to ask what was wrong. Lottie missed her father. Thanksgiving had come and gone and she hadn't heard one word from him. Now Christmas was coming. And her birthday, too, which was in January. I knew Lottie was afraid he wouldn't remember either day. But he would. Of course he would.

"Should I give this to my niece, Maryanne?" Mrs. Thrasher asked. She was holding up a diary with a red plaid cover. "Or this one?" She showed me a white one.

I shrugged. "I'd like plaid, but maybe she's different."

"No, she's just like you," Mrs. Thrasher said. "Sort of giggly and funny." She handed the plaid diary to the clerk.

Mrs. Thrasher thought I was giggly and funny? I looked at myself in the mirror behind the counter. My mouth turned up naturally at the corners, but I wasn't smiling. Actually I was close to crying. Or kicking something.

I shouldn't have come with them, I thought. I needed time alone to prepare for the idea of Christmas coming around again—for the second time without Dad.

(Unless he's out there, looking, wondering about us, lost in the dark . . . Oh, Dad, please. Make this turn out to be only a bad dream.)

"Are you okay, Maryanne?" Mrs. Thrasher asked anxiously.

She was no taller than I was, and so she looked directly into my tear-stung eyes.

"Oh, little girl," Mrs. Thrasher said suddenly, and she reached out and hugged me hard. "It gets easier," she whispered in my ear. "Honestly. I promise."

But I didn't believe her. Life had only gotten harder as I'd gotten older. And I didn't believe in Santa anymore.

The next evening Mom astonished me by telling me she was going to a concert with the man who owned the bookstore across the street from the espresso shop.

"His mother bought the tickets so she and her neighbor could go," Mom said as she yanked a comb through her hair in front of the bathroom mirror. She had already changed into a black suit and high-heeled shoes. "But both of them came down with colds, so Stephen—Mr. Barker—asked me if I'd like to go. Wasn't that nice of him?"

"I guess so," I said uncomfortably. "How do you know him? I haven't seen him around. What does Mrs. Hale say?"

Mom put on lipstick carefully, then said, "He comes

into the shop in the afternoons a lot—you've probably seen him. And Margaret's known him for years. She says he's awfully nice."

She was using the word "nice" again. I shifted from one foot to the other. Was this a date?

"How do I look?" Mom asked. "I'm getting fat. I look terrible, don't I?"

"You aren't fat," I said.

"Should I wear something else?" Mom asked.

I shrugged. "You look fine. But what am I supposed to do? We always spend Sunday nights together watching TV."

"Ask Lottie to come over," Mom said. "How about renting a movie? Do you want to do that?"

"I guess so," I said. "This just seems so sudden. What time will you be home?"

"Well, it is sudden because his mother just decided she was too sick to go. We'll be home at ten-thirty at the latest," Mom said. She was scowling at herself in the mirror.

The doorbell rang and she ran to answer it. "Here's Mr. Barker," she called to me. "Come and meet him."

"I'm in the bathroom. I'll have to see him some other time," I called back, and I shut the bathroom door. I *was* feeling kind of sick.

Mom left, calling out good-bye and sounding embarrassed, saying she'd phone me during intermission.

What was going on? I'd been in the bookstore several times, but I'd never noticed a man there, and I'd

75

been waited on by an older woman who wore thick glasses. Who was this Mr. Barker and what did he want with my mother? And what did she want with him?

I sat on the love seat with Jimmy and tried to take in this new wrinkle in our lives. But I couldn't. It was too strange.

"I should have told her she looked fat," I said to him. "I bet she wouldn't have gone out with him."

Maybe, Jimmy seemed to say. But don't bet on it.

# Chapter Seven

Mom and Mrs. Hale worked longer hours in December, both at the Arms and at the espresso shop, so I didn't see much of Mom, and neither did Mr. Barker, I hoped. Lottie and I spent almost every afternoon and evening together. On Saturday mornings we took care of Monica and Audrey. On Saturday afternoons, we carried Mrs. Thrasher's shopping home and ran errands for her and several of her friends who lived in the Other Arm. By the week before Christmas, I was practically rich.

"I've had a new brainstorm about Mom's present," I told Lottie on the last Sunday. "I saw a ficus tree at the nursery on the boulevard. You know—it looks like an outdoor tree, only smaller. I bet she'd love having it. She likes the one in the library, and this one's nicer."

We were walking through Westlake Center downtown, window-shopping and watching the crowds. The escalators were so crowded we had to wait in line at each level, but we didn't mind. Christmas would be over soon enough, and then dreary old January would set in.

"So you gave up on the idea of that necklace we saw?" Lottie asked me.

I grimaced. "Maybe I shouldn't have. Maybe she'd like the necklace better."

"Your mom doesn't have anyplace to wear the necklace," Lottie said. "Think about it. She doesn't wear jewelry around the Arms or the espresso shop. And she hardly ever goes out anywhere."

"I know," I said. Mom had only gone out with Mr. Barker once, and that probably wouldn't happen again. "But I still haven't figured out how to get the tree home. It's too big to carry and they don't deliver."

"Tom can help us take it home in Monica's wagon," Lottie said. "It's only six or seven blocks."

"And then where do I keep it until Christmas?" I asked. "Mom runs in and out of your apartment all the time. And the tree wouldn't be safe at Tom's, not unless Monica goes to the penitentiary before then."

"Mrs. Thrasher can keep it for you. I know she will. If you give your mom the tree, then my mom and I can give her a big fancy pot for it. Perfect, right?"

I was being bumped and jostled by some serious

shoppers, so I moved on. "Let me look at the necklace once more," I said. "And then we've got to start home."

We visited the craft shop again and studied the necklace carefully. I knew Mom would like it. But Lottie was right—she'd never wear it. And she'd love having her own tree.

"What do you think?" Lottie asked.

"I'll get the tree," I told her.

"Next year maybe things will be different," Lottie said. "You'll live in a house and have dozens of trees. And your mom will have a place to wear a great necklace. Maybe she'll even have a date with somebody."

I shook my head emphatically. "She won't. Not ever. Not a real date."

We took the bus back to our own neighborhood and stopped at the nursery, and I watched carefully while the salesman put a red "sold" tag on the world's most gorgeous ficus tree.

I promised him I'd take it out of the store in the next couple of days, but I wasn't all that certain about Lottie's plans. We could count on Mrs. Thrasher going along with just about anything, but Tom was another matter. He was flirting with detention all the time because of his war with the cafeteria.

"You'll starve before they change the food," I'd told him one day after school.

"Then they'll have a new problem," Tom had said. "A dead body in the cafeteria."

"What makes you think they'd even notice?" I had said. Both of us laughed at that. But if Tom did anything else and got detention during that last week before Christmas vacation, he wouldn't be available to haul the tree in Monica's wagon. That could be a problem.

The next afternoon Tom agreed to help before dinner, but when we got home, we saw another of his mother's banners hanging from the balcony. It read: "Tom, something is living under your bed."

"Haven't you cleaned up your bedroom yet?" I asked.

His face burned red. "I'll haul your tree home tomorrow," he said.

"You want a big stick?" I asked.

"What for?"

"To kill what's living under your bed," I said.

He gave me a warning look and shot ahead of me into the lobby.

"I guess I'd better not tease him," I told Lottie while we climbed the steps.

"Good thinking," Lottie said. "We need everything to fall into place this week, or we'll end up hauling that monstrous tree home ourselves in Mrs. Thrasher's shopping cart."

"I already thought of that," I said. "It won't fit."

We had to wait for the elevator to come back down, since Tom had beaten us to it and didn't hold it for us. Martie skulked in the front door behind us, took one look at us, and headed down the hall.

"She invited Dolly to go ice-skating with her," Lottie said, watching her walk away.

"Really? Is Dolly going?" I wanted to learn, but I wasn't sure I'd want to be anywhere near Martie.

Lottie shrugged. "She didn't say. Dolly and I used to go together all the time."

"She likes you better than Martie," I offered.

"That's not saying much," Lottie said, laughing. "Even Monica likes me better, and she hates everybody."

The elevator door slid back and we got in. Someone had hung a wreath on the elevator wall, and it smelled wonderful.

"Christmas is almost here," Lottie said.

I hugged myself, thinking of the ficus tree. Maybe I'd hang some ornaments on it, just for fun. And tie a red ribbon around the trunk. Mom was going to be so surprised.

The next afternoon was cold and dark, but no snow fell, so I was sure Tom, Lottie, and I could get the tree home without any problems. We checked to make sure Mrs. Thrasher was home before we left the building. Mom was at the shop and would be until six. I was finally getting into the Christmas spirit.

It took Tom and me both to lift the tree while Lottie held the wagon still. We had trouble getting the tree out the nursery door because it was so tall, and I winced when I saw a shower of leaves fall as we tried to pull the tree through at an angle, all without dropping it.

"Is it ruined?" I cried.

Tom, who was the tallest, reached up and pulled off a loose leaf. "It's not so bad."

I looked up. "We've got to be more careful."

Traffic was terrible, and we barely made it across the street with the wagon before the light changed.

"That bus nearly squashed the tree," I complained to Tom.

"It nearly squashed us, you mean," he said. "I didn't know the thing was going to be so heavy."

"Neither did I," I said. He was pulling the wagon, I was pushing, and Lottie was keeping the tree steady.

"One more intersection and we've got it home," Tom said.

We had barely moved the wagon out into the street when somebody in a yellow car turned the corner too fast.

"Look out!" Tom yelled, and he yanked hard on the wagon to get it out of the way. The car sped past just as the wagon tipped over. I watched, horrified, as the tree fell into the street in spite of Lottie's efforts to hang on to it.

Tom turned the wagon upright while Lottie and I struggled with the tree. Most of the dirt had spilled out of the pot, and I knelt to scrape it up, but another car honked at me.

"Maryanne, we've got to get out of the way," Lottie said.

A truck honked. Tom pulled the wagon toward the curb, dodging cars and looking back at us. Lottie and I lifted the tree and hurried behind him.

When we put the tree back in its pot, I patted the roots down and tried not to cry.

"We can get more dirt, Russell," Tom said. "Don't freak out on me. We'll get some out of the back flower bed at the Arm."

"But the branches," I wailed. Some were broken. I tried to push them up in place but they flopped down again.

"We'll cut them off," Lottie said. "Or we'll ask Mrs. Thrasher to do it. She knows lots about gardening. She'll know what to do."

We got the tree into Mrs. Thrasher's apartment without any more trouble. But even though Tom replaced all the dirt and Mrs. Thrasher pruned off the broken branches, I was afraid it didn't look good enough.

"Your mom will still love it," Lottie said.

It was better than no tree at all, I told myself. But still, I'd meant to do better. I needed the tree as much as Mom did. Maybe even more.

On Christmas Eve, we went to the neighborhood church with Lottie and her mom. The night was cold and clear, and most of the houses and apartment buildings we passed were decorated for Christmas. The air smelled of damp evergreens and wood smoke.

On the way home, Mom and Mrs. Hale walked ahead, talking and laughing together. Lottie and I followed, quietly, with our hands shoved in our pockets.

"My dad hasn't called," Lottie said. "We've left the answering machine on all the time."

"He probably will tonight," I said. "It's early yet."

"He won't," Lottie said.

"Then why don't you call him?" I asked. "You have his number, don't you?"

Lottie waited so long to answer that I knew what she would say. "No," she said. "He has an unlisted number. His wife wants it that way. Or that's what he said, anyway."

I looked down, pretending to concentrate on my feet. "When was the last time he called you?" I asked.

"Last June," Lottie said. "He won't call tonight or tomorrow. He doesn't remember me. Or he wishes he didn't."

Lottie wasn't crying. She said the terrible words in a normal voice, as if she were talking about the weather.

"I'm sure you're wrong," I said. "Maybe he's tried to call lots of times when you didn't have the answering machine turned on."

"He could write. He could answer my letters."

We were passing the Castle. The tree in the bay window was lighted, and the roses in the stained-glass window glowed like coals. Our mothers were half a block ahead, still chattering and laughing, but we caught up with them and I pointed back at the wonderful house.

"Look at the house, Mom," I said. "Isn't it beautiful? Don't you wish it belonged to us?"

Mom looked back and I saw her smile. "I'd have to win the lottery," she said.

"Someday we're going to have a house like that," I said. "Maybe even a better one."

"Someday, baby," Mom said. She walked on with Mrs. Hale then and didn't look back.

Lottie and I linked arms and walked home to share Christmas Eve together. She was the best friend I'd ever had, and it broke my heart to see her so unhappy. But I didn't know how to fix things for her, the way she fixed things when I needed to move a tree home. Some problems were too big.

Lottie, her mother, and I moved the tree from Mrs. Thrasher's apartment to mine as soon as we got home. Mrs. Thrasher, who'd been waiting, left to spend Christmas with her friends in the retirement village.

"What's this?" Mom asked as we dragged the tree through the apartment door.

"Merry Christmas," I told her.

The look on Mom's face was worth all the worrying and trouble. "It's beautiful," she said. She circled the tree, touching the branches and the decorations. "It's wonderful. I missed having something green of my own, and here it is. Thank you, Maryanne."

Jimmy circled the tree, too, his eyes huge. I realized then that he missed trees as much as we did.

We *need* a house, I thought. A yard. We really do.

We ate a late supper in Lottie's apartment. Afterward I opened the gift Lottie had given me, a picture of the two of us in a frame that looked like mother-of-pearl. I gave her a tape of her favorite group. All over the building, radios played Christmas carols. Altogether, it was a nice Christmas Eve.

But Lottie's father never called.

The next day Tom came to my door shortly after breakfast and handed me a small, square box.

"Merry Christmas, Russell," he said, and he walked away before I could say anything more than "Thanks."

I hadn't thought of getting anything for him, and I was embarrassed. While Mom watched, I unwrapped his gift, and found a wood carving of a seagull. It was small and a little crude, but there was something wonderfully graceful about the spread wings and the way the gull's neck was stretched out, as if it could take flight any moment.

"Tom made that?" Mom asked. "For heaven's sake. It's quite good, isn't it?"

I shook my head, marveling over the carving. I never suspected that Tom might be artistic in any way. But even if I had I certainly wouldn't have expected him to let me find out about it.

"He likes seagulls," I told Mom.

"Well, I guess he does!" Mom said.

I put the seagull on my bedroom windowsill beside the picture Lottie had given me. I couldn't bear to set anything on the dresser where the unicorn had been. Not yet. Not as long as we lived here.

Suddenly I opened my closet and pushed back my clothes. All my crazy words were still there, scribbled all over the closet wall. Neither Mom nor I ever mentioned them—or how crazy I'd acted that night.

We didn't really talk about disturbing things like that night, or her date with Mr. Barker. We sort of pretended nothing had happened and went on as before. We'd both gotten pretty good at pretending since Dad had died.

Sometimes I thought of cleaning the words off the wall—the ink was washable. But I didn't do it, because a part of me thought I'd never get away from this place.

The gifts Mom had given me were scattered on the bed—a new sweater, new jeans, two new shirts—clothes Dad had never seen.

I shut the closet door and took the remains of my music box out of the drawer. While it played, I looked at the poster of trees taped to the wall.

"Merry Christmas, Daddy," I whispered.

# Chapter Eight

When school started again after Christmas break, I realized I didn't feel like a stranger there any longer. I knew almost as many of the seventh graders as Lottie, and I had a special place to sit during lunch, a place the other kids always saved for me.

But there was one person I would have been happier not knowing—Martie. The holiday hadn't mellowed her, I thought when I saw her staring at me outside our language class. She probably hated Christmas.

"*What*," I said defensively.

"Your new shirt is really ugly," Martie said. "I hate the way it bunches up around your neck."

I could have lived through that, but Martie said it in front of some of the girls who had new clothes all the time, the girls Martie was always trying to make friends with. Most of them laughed.

I blushed so hard I wondered if my face would burst into flame. "At least my head doesn't grow to a point, Martie," I yelled as I pushed past her.

Martie's face turned red, too, and the other girls laughed again. Martie's relationship with them seemed pretty uncertain even at the best of times, and they were as willing to snub her as they were me.

"You're as good as dead," Lottie whispered to me as Martie stormed to her seat, her nose in the air. "She'll get even."

"What can she do to me that she hasn't done a million times before?" I asked.

But Martie told her mother what I'd said, and Mrs. Eldrich told Mom I was mean and cruel and ought to be punished. This could have been bad news, but Mom laughed when she told me, and added, "Way to go, kiddo. You're learning."

Maybe the situation wouldn't have been funny to us if Mom hadn't quit her job at the Arms that week, thanks to the extra hours she was getting at the espresso shop. To celebrate, we ate out at a nice restaurant—for the first time in too long to remember. While I chose dessert, I thought we were doing so well, who knew what might happen next?

Lottie's thirteenth birthday was not such a happy occasion. Mrs. Hale sent us downtown to a movie in the afternoon and then served cake and ice cream to us when we got home. Lottie said very little and hardly smiled, and I knew why. She hadn't seen her father for months.

"But he sent me this," Lottie explained. She showed me a manicure set.

"It's just great," I said as enthusiastically as I could. I'd seen the crumpled Christmas wrapping in the wastepaper basket in the corner.

Afterward I told Mom, "The manicure set was the gift he didn't bother giving her at Christmas. I bet he doesn't even remember how old she is."

Mom bit her lip. "I have an awful feeling you're right."

But Lottie never complained, and the next time I saw her bedroom, the manicure set sat on top of the dresser beside a framed snapshot of a very young Lottie with her father, standing in the snow somewhere.

Dolly's parents had given her new skates for Christmas, and Lottie and I went with her to the ice rink one Sunday afternoon after lunch so that she could try them out. While I wobbled around the edge of the ice on my rented skates, Lottie and Dolly twirled in the middle with the other experts.

Finally Lottie took pity on me and flashed over to where I was hanging on to the side railing. "You aren't having much fun, are you? Hold on to me and I'll take you around a couple of times."

I was about to agree when Lottie froze. "Oh, no. Here's Tom and Vic. And Martie's with them, but I bet they didn't ride on the bus together. Vic hates Martie more than Tom does."

I craned my neck so that I could see Tom and his friend gliding out on the ice. Martie hung on to the railing, glaring at Dolly.

"Tom can skate, but I don't think Vic can," Lottie said. "I've never seen him here before. But Martie used to come with Dolly all the time."

"Before you moved in," I added.

"I wish Martie could get in with the in crowd and leave everybody else alone."

"Martie'll never get in with that crowd," I said. "They don't make friends with anybody who doesn't live in places like theirs. At least, they don't make after-school friends with them. But you know what? Martie told me her mother is looking for another apartment for them to live in."

"She lies," Lottie said. "Her mother has to stay and work at the Arms. She'd never move anywhere else. Hey, look at Tom."

Tom had joined Dolly and they were skating to-gether. Vic bumbled around on the edges of the ice, trying his best, but he spent most of his time on his rear with his mouth open and tears in his eyes.

"Tom's a good skater," I said.

"See how he skates with Dolly?" Lottie said. "They've done that lots of times. He's ice-dancing, but if you told him that, he'd blow up."

"They look great together," I said, trying not to

choke on my envy. "Dolly's nice and she deserves to have everything, including a boyfriend. If that's what Tom is."

"They're old pals," Lottie said. "That's all. I know for an absolute fact that Dolly likes one of the eighth-grade boys."

The eighth graders seemed so old and mysterious to me that I couldn't imagine why Dolly might be interested in one of them. But I felt relieved—until I wondered why I cared one way or the other.

During January, two of the waitresses at the espresso shop quit, and Mom and Mrs. Hale began working full-time, five days a week. They took turns coming home to fix dinner for Lottie and me. It was a good thing Lottie and I got along so well together, because we were practically living in each other's pockets.

Twice, when things at the shop got busy and neither of our mothers could leave, old Mr. Penn had pizza delivered to us. We wrote him a thank-you note each time.

"Mr. Penn had tears in his eyes when he read the note," Mom told me the first time.

I gawked at her. "What for? It was nice of him to send the pizza. I'd never had four kinds of cheese before."

"His grandchildren are beastly," Mom said. "No matter what he does, they never thank him. He thinks you two are perfect."

"If he only knew," I said.

"You and Lottie are really close, aren't you?" Mom asked.

"We'd better be," I said. "We spend all our time together."

Mom made that little humming sound that meant she was thinking. "Margaret and I have been talking about something. We haven't decided yet, but we want to take over the shop from Mr. Penn. He plans to move to Arizona, and he's going to sell the place to somebody—and he'd like it to be us."

"Where would you get the money?" I asked. My mouth was dry. "It must cost a lot."

"I'll use our savings as a down payment. Then he said we could make small payments to him instead of big payments to a bank," Mom said.

"But what if something goes wrong?" I asked. "What if you can't do enough business to stay open? The sandwich shop down the street closed. And remember what happened to Dad's electronics store. Remember how—"

"I remember," Mom said. She avoided looking at me. "This is different. The espresso shop has been there for a long time and it's very popular. The sandwich shop—well, Mr. Penn said they charged too much and the food wasn't very good."

"But Dad's store—" I began.

"Times were harder then," Mom said. "It was a different kind of business."

Now she looked straight at me. "Margaret and I are sure we can do this. She's worked in the shop for two years, and before that she managed a restaurant, so she knows more about the business than I do. I can keep books and handle the money. We believe we can do this together. And so does Mr. Penn. He wants to help us any way he can."

I remembered when Dad's store began to fail, the long hours he worked, the way he grew so tired.

"Mom, please don't," I whispered.

"I need to do this," Mom said. "I need to prove to myself that I can make a good life for us."

"But couldn't you just run the shop for Mr. Penn after he moves? We could buy a house and have a good life that way!" I cried. "Wouldn't that be better?"

"It's not the same thing," Mom said. "Mr. Penn wants to sell the shop and I want to *own* it, not just work there. We'll live in a house again, I promise. But now I have to do this. I hoped you'd be glad."

"I can't," I said. "I'm sorry." My eyes burned with tears. "I'm too scared to be glad."

On the following Saturday, Lottie and I helped Mrs. Thrasher load her furniture into a truck rented by her friends from the retirement village. She was moving into the apartment she had wanted for so long.

The excitement Mrs. Thrasher felt was catching. "This will be me someday," I told Lottie. "It could have been me sooner if Mom hadn't decided to use our savings on the shop."

Lottie, shoving a cardboard box into the truck, looked back at me. "But don't you think it's exciting that they'll have their own business?"

I shrugged. "I'd rather we had our own house."

"Someday you will," Lottie said. She gave the box a final shove. "Someday we'll both have everything we want, Maryanne."

I didn't answer.

Even Monica made herself useful to Mrs. Thrasher and didn't break or steal anything. Tom and a man from the first floor brought down the heaviest pieces, and promised to follow the truck and help unload it.

"Did Mrs. Eldrich give you back your deposit?" I asked Mrs. Thrasher. The manager had never been known to return a deposit.

"She said she wouldn't," Mrs. Thrasher said indignantly, "so I didn't clean one thing, especially not the oven. I would have cleaned it if your mothers were still working here, but when I heard Eldrich couldn't find anybody to replace them and was doing the work herself, I decided to leave the mess right where it was. Revenge is sweetest when it's stuck to the oven racks, I always say."

When the loading was finished, we waved good-bye until Mrs. Thrasher and her belongings were out of sight.

"I'm glad she's happy, but I'll miss her," I said.

"It's sort of like having somebody in the family

move away," Lottie said. "I hardly ever see my grandmother, and Mrs. Thrasher took her place."

"Maybe she'll come back to visit," I said.

"Would you?" Lottie asked, laughing.

I laughed, too. "Only to throw rocks at the windows."

The employees at the espresso shop gave Mr. Penn a party the night before he left for Arizona. Snow had fallen all day, and the few customers who came in were glad to share in the celebration. After the other shops on the street closed, the owners and workers came in, too, to say good-bye to the old man they had known so many years.

For the first time I spoke to Stephen Barker, the owner of the bookstore across the street. He was a thin man with a shy, crooked smile, and he seemed to know both Mrs. Hale and Mom quite well. He'd come with the two clerks who worked for him, and they gave Mr. Penn a carton of books to take with him to his new home.

"Do you like to read?" Mr. Barker asked me when we found ourselves standing together.

"Sure," I said. "I check two books out of the library every week." Then, realizing what I'd said, I added, "I'd like to *own* lots of books, but . . . I do own some books that I bought and people gave me, but now, well . . ."

Finally I gave up. He made me so nervous I was

sorry I hadn't run off when he first spoke to me.

He blinked at me through his glasses and said, "Books are expensive, aren't they? I'm glad you go to the library. It was one of my favorite places when I was your age."

I could see no way of rescuing myself from this awkward conversation, and I was panicking when I heard Mom say, "I can't believe this place is really ours."

I smiled vaguely at Mr. Barker and hurried away to stand beside her before he had a chance to say anything else. I didn't share Mom's pleasure—I remembered how happy my parents had been when Dad opened his store—but I was more than willing to pretend I was happy if I could escape from Mr. Barker.

Later, when I thought I wouldn't be noticed, I looked back at him—and saw him watching Mom. He wore a small, quiet smile, as if he was seeing something that pleased him very much.

No, no, I thought. No. Maybe he took Mom to that concert, but it was only because he had the tickets and nobody else would go with him.

But a week later Mom took a night off and went to a movie with Mr. Barker. He came to the apartment to pick her up and brought me a video of my favorite movie musical.

"I like this one, too," he told me while he waited awkwardly in the living room for Mom, who was taking forever to get her coat. "I've seen it many times."

I fidgeted. "Thanks, but you didn't have to do this."

"I didn't want you to be lonely tonight," he said. "You could come out to the movies with us." His voice sounded almost sincere but I was too horrified to look at his face and check his expression.

"No," I managed to gasp. "I'm practically thirteen."

Mom rescued me by coming back with her coat. After they left, I ran down the hall to Lottie's.

"I feel as if I'm in the middle of a bad dream," I complained. "My own mother! She's forty, Lottie. That's too old to be going out on dates."

"Mom told me they were going to a movie," Lottie admitted. "I was afraid to say anything to you."

My face stung with a blush. "What else did your mom say?"

Lottie looked everywhere but at me. "Only that she thinks it's cute, especially since Mr. Barker doesn't mind that your mom is older than he is."

"Older!" I cried. "She's older? This is awful. It's disgusting! Is she crazy?"

"She's only three years older," Lottie said. "That's not so much."

I stared. "Lottie, think! You're three years older than Dolly's repulsive little brother. Do you want to go to a movie with him?"

"I'd rather die," Lottie said. "Gosh, I never thought of it that way."

"Just promise you won't tell anybody," I said. "If Martie finds out my mother went out with somebody young, I'll run away from home."

"He's not exactly *young*," Lottie protested. "Nobody his age could be called young, Maryanne."

"Young, old, who cares?" I said. "They're both too old to date." I gnawed on my thumbnail until it hurt. "I sure hope they took the stairs. If Monica's robbing people in the elevator again, she'll see them and blab it all over the building."

Lottie came back to my apartment and we watched the video. But I couldn't concentrate. All I could think about was what I'd do if somebody I knew saw Mom and Mr. Barker somewhere and asked me about them.

"I'll say he's her brother," I said aloud.

"What?" Lottie asked, her eyes on the screen. "What?"

"Nothing," I said. "Here. Have the last cookie. I'm not hungry anymore."

# Chapter Nine

In March, the flower beds at the Castle were crowded with yellow and blue crocuses, and I made Lottie stop every morning while I looked at them. The branches on the willow tree beside the house showed small pale buds, not yet ready to unfold into leaves, but the promise was there. Sometimes I could hardly bear to look, but I couldn't pass by, either. The last spring had been difficult, and I hadn't thought of gardening with Dad then because I still missed him so much. Now I couldn't keep gardening off my mind.

If Dad had still been alive, we'd have looked through seed catalogs in the evenings while we sat together at the dining room table. On weekends we'd have worked in the garden, turning the soil, making plans to plant carrots here, lettuce there, and maybe even try potatoes again, just for fun, even though we'd never raised any that were any larger than marbles.

"You've got the Russell family green thumb," Dad had told me more than once. "Now we have to make sure your mother doesn't get too close to the seedlings, because she could kill them with one look."

Mom had always laughed at that, but Dad had been right. Mom had tried, but Dad had been the expert.

Planting a garden sounded like more fun than the school dance planned for the first day of spring, although Lottie didn't agree.

"I don't know why you aren't excited," she complained on the way home one afternoon. "Don't you want a new dress for the dance? You could buy one, but there's still time to make one if you hurry. I'm done with mine, and I can help you."

"I can't sew," I said. "I keep telling you that, but you don't want to believe me. I've got enough saved to buy a dress for the dance, so why should I make one?"

"Because it's creative," Lottie said. "Don't you want to make something with your own hands?"

"I want to plant flowers with my own hands," I said. "In fact, I'll use my money for a big planter for the balcony. I'll wear my bathrobe to the dance."

"Here we go again," Lottie said, laughing. "Farmer Russell."

"Look," I said, interrupting the argument. "There's Martie. How did she get home so fast without passing us?"

"She goes another way, so she can walk a couple of

blocks with the in kids before they cross the boule-vard," Lottie said. "They're having a party after the dance and she wants to be invited."

"Who cares about them?" I said. "We could have our own party."

"Who'd come?" Lottie asked, practical as always.

"You're right," I said. "Anyway, who has room? You couldn't give a real party in one of our apartments."

"Then we'll wait until you move into a house," Lottie said.

Sure, I thought. There's no chance of that. Mom doesn't even talk about it.

On Saturday afternoon, I bought a planter at the nursery and filled it with yellow primroses. They'd never see sunlight, but at least they would bloom for a while. Jimmy watched me with big, round eyes as I arranged it on the balcony. Let me out to help, he seemed to beg. I promise I won't jump off the railing.

I caught him as he tried to escape when I came back inside. "Forget it," I told him. "You have to enjoy the flowers from this side of the glass."

Spring wasn't much fun for me or my cat, I thought.

I made up my mind to bring up the subject of a house again to Mom. When the time was right. In the meantime, I added to my collection of house pictures. The shoe box was half full.

And sometimes I sat on my closet floor and looked at the words I'd scribbled on the wall.

The seventh-grade girls always hoped each after-school dance would be different from the earlier ones, but we were always disappointed. At the spring dance, the boys huddled together as they'd done every other time, in whispering, snickering knots on one side of the gym close to the food tables. They'd been forced to at least come inside the gym instead of standing in the hall, but that was the extent of the progress between fall and spring. The girls knew we would eventually dance with each other, if we danced at all.

"I already hate this and we've only been here half an hour," Lottie said. "I went to all this work making a new dress and nobody cares—except the girls."

The gym was overheated and smelled of dust and old sneakers. The dance committee's attempts at decoration had not been a big success, and yellow and white streamers already were coming loose and sagging. Everybody looked grim, as if they were all waiting in the dentist's office.

"Boys don't care about dresses," I said. I wore jeans and a pink sweater, and wished I'd worn my bathrobe, to liven things up.

"Boys don't care about anything except food," Lottie said. "Look at them gobbling up everything."

"Why don't you walk over and ask one of them to dance?" I gave Lottie a little shove. "Go on, ask Tom. I bet he'll dance with you."

"Not even if I paid him," Lottie said.

"Then ask somebody else," I insisted.

"Who, Vic?" Lottie scoffed. "Or one of the teachers?"

I watched Tom open another soft drink can. "Hmm," I said.

"You sound exactly like your mother," Lottie said, laughing. "What are you thinking?"

"That Tom doesn't have anything to do," I said. I pulled my hands out of my pockets, took a deep breath, and marched across the room to stand directly in front of Tom.

"Put down the pop and dance with me," I said.

Tom stared. "Are you nuts, Russell?" he demanded. "Why would I do something like that?"

Vic laughed nervously. "Who put you up to this, Maryanne? Lottie? This sounds like one of her ideas. How much is she paying you to dance with Tom?"

"Nobody's paying me anything," I said. "I'm doing it for free, to get things started here."

Tom's face turned scarlet. "I don't want to dance with a girl."

"Well, who are you going to dance with, then?" I demanded. "Vic?"

"I'm not dancing with anybody!" Tom exclaimed.

"This is a dance, so everybody *should* dance," I argued.

"Jeez, Russell, you're such a pain," Tom said.

I took his soft drink can away and handed it to Vic.

"Come on," I said to Tom. "Start dancing right now. If you do it, all the other boys will, too."

"The other guys will beat me up on the way home," Tom said.

"Are you going to leave me standing here so Martie Eldrich and her snotty friends can laugh at me?" I asked.

Tom looked around, located Martie, and growled, "Aw, jeez, Russell, you cheater. You know how I hate her. You're doing this to ruin my life."

"No, I'm just embarrassed," I said. "I wish I hadn't come over here and asked you, but now I have, and if you don't dance with me, Martie will laugh about it for the rest of my life."

"Come on, then," Tom said, pulling me out a few feet onto the floor. "But I don't know how to dance so don't blame me if you end up looking really stupid. Maybe you'll be crippled for life after I break your big flapping feet."

"Thank you, Prince Charming," I said. I was sorry I had even thought Tom might be willing to dance. And even sorrier that I was making an idiot of myself in front of everybody. But the deed was done. Clumsy as he was, Tom was dancing with me.

"I think I'll kill you on the way home, Russell," Tom said when the song was over.

"Don't bother," I said. "I'm going to slit my wrists all by myself." I turned and walked away from him, my

105

face red, but I kept smiling even though the smile actually hurt.

"That was incredible," Lottie whispered. "You're the first girl in the seventh grade to ever dance with a boy at a school dance."

"Wonderful," I said bitterly. "Let's go home right now before I sick up on my good sweater and really make myself famous."

We left and walked most of the way home in silence. Finally Lottie said, "Whose idea was it to have dances after school?"

"Probably the cafeteria workers," I said. "I think everybody agrees they hate us."

"No, I bet it was the guidance counselors," Lottie said. "They do stuff like that. They're supposed to make us well-adjusted."

"So how come the boy I danced with threatened to kill me on the way home?" I asked.

There was a small silence, and then Lottie began giggling. Unwillingly, I joined in, until finally we stopped walking and hung on to each other, screaming with laughter.

"My mother told me these were the best years of my life," Lottie said, gasping.

"Bummer," I said. "I can hardly wait for high school. Do you think it gets better?"

"Don't count on it," Lottie said. "This may have been a preview of coming attractions, like in the movies."

Several times when I walked to the espresso shop after school to talk to Mom, I found Mr. Barker there, sitting alone at a small table in the corner by the window. The first few times I refused to let myself brood about it, but one day I saw him watching Mom again, smiling his shy crooked smile, and I decided he liked Mom too much. Much too much, considering how old she was. Didn't he notice that she had at least two dozen gray hairs?

I looked away and tried to organize my thinking, but ideas were colliding in my mind and I couldn't decide if I was embarrassed or angry or both. Finally I gave way to anger.

What did he mean, hanging around in the shop when he ought to be taking care of his own store? Why was he smiling at Mom like that? Did she know? Did she care?

Maybe, I decided, I'd better say something about this problem to Mom. But I couldn't bring myself to do it. This was one of those disturbing issues we tended to avoid. Mom would probably be embarrassed. I remembered how I'd felt in fifth grade when Jack Larson, a fourth grader, had a really stupid crush on me and trailed me around like a shadow. I'd done everything I could think of to discourage him so that I could put a stop to the other kids' teasing. Nothing worked.

What did Mrs. Hale think about this? Was she

laughing at Mom?

Maybe I should say something to Mr. Barker himself. No. That would be impossible. Every time he tried to talk to me, my mouth went dry and my ears rang.

There had to be a way to put an end to this, if Mom didn't do it herself. I didn't even let myself think about the possiblity that Mom might like him back.

I stayed away from the shop after that, even though Mom said she missed the after-school visits. And when Lottie wanted to drop in, I made an excuse to go home.

I won't put up with this, I told myself. But I wasn't sure what it was I didn't want to put up with. Mom went to movies with Mr. Barker regularly, and I didn't like it one bit. But I *hated* the way he looked at her.

In addition to baby-sitting the Kingsley girls with me Saturday mornings, Lottie took care of a girl on the second floor on Tuesday evenings when her parents went to a class at the community college. I hoped to find a regular job like Lottie's, but so far no one had responded to the notice I'd put up on the lobby bulletin board.

One of Mrs. Thrasher's friends who still lived at the Other Arm hired me to vacuum for her every Saturday afternoon. Mom barely approved, hummed a lot, and finally told me that it reminded her too much of the time she'd spent working for Mrs. Eldrich.

"But Mrs. Burke is nice," I said. I was helping Mom

change sheets in the bedrooms that evening, and I looked up from the blanket I was smoothing in place. "She's better than nice. She pays me and then says thank you about a million times."

"Gee," Mom said. "Pay and gratitude both. That's more than I ever got from Mrs. Eldrich."

"Then is it okay if I keep on working for Mrs. Burke?"

Mom hummed a little more as she flapped the bedspread over the bed. "Well, maybe. For a while."

"Why only a while?" I asked. "She's counting on me."

"We'll see," Mom said vaguely. "Don't make her any long-term promises, okay?"

"But why?" I persisted.

But Mom hurried out of the room carrying an armload of sheets and didn't answer. Did her silence mean something?

❧

March passed and April came, warmer than usual, with bright blue skies and sweet-scented winds. The willow tree at the Castle was draped with pale green leaves, and the old cherry trees held up white blossoms to the sun. Once when I saw a weed thrusting up through the dark earth, I ran across the lawn and pulled it out. The smell of fresh earth on my hand made me almost sick with longing.

I *need* a garden, I thought—I need to work outside, and not just with a planter full of dying primroses. I hate not having a house. I hate it so much I think I would do anything to get out of the apartment.

I blinked furiously to keep away tears and hurried home, staring straight ahead.

"Greetings, Russell!"

I looked up and saw Tom hanging out over his balcony railing. "Look up!" Tom yelled. "Look!"

I raised my head and saw the gulls overhead, riding the winds, their bright white wings stretched out in the sun. There were so many, and they were so beautiful, that for a moment I could scarcely breathe.

"Come on up here and look at them the right way," Tom called down to me. "My door's open and Monica isn't here. Come on."

At first I shook my head, but then changed my mind and went on up to his apartment. He was hanging so far over the edge of his balcony railing that he scared me.

"You ought to be careful," I said.

"I am careful," he argued. He swung himself in, grasping the post with both hands, and then jumped to the deck. "Come on. I'll hang on to your legs. Lean back and out, and then look straight up. It seems almost as if you could fly with the gulls. Try it."

I dropped my books and sat on the edge of the railing, holding the post with one hand. Tom grabbed my knees and told me to let go and lean back.

"Trust me," he said. "Grab the railing. I'll keep you

from going over backward."

Ordinarily I wouldn't have trusted him for any-thing, but there was something about his expression that let me feel willing to put myself in his hands, just this once. I let go of the post, gripped the railing with both hands, and leaned back.

I looked straight up. It was magical. All I saw was the blue sky filled with wheeling, crying gulls. I felt free—delicately balanced above the city, above every-thing that was shabby, and the white wings stretched and wheeled over me. Free.

Tom yanked on my knees, pulling me forward. "You're heavier than I thought you were, Russell. Time's up."

I stood up, almost dizzy, unable to stop smiling. "That was wonderful," I said. "That's the best thing I ever saw."

"Now I bet you wish you were a bird."

"How did you know?" I asked.

"Because I know what a jerk you are," he said, his voice gruff. He turned his back on me and pushed open the glass door leading into his apartment.

I followed him inside reluctantly. I looked back once, and only saw the shabby tan building across the street.

"I've got stuff to do, Russell," Tom said. He yanked open the door to the hall. "See you later."

I stopped in the doorway. "Thanks, Tom."

Tom grinned suddenly. "Great, wasn't it?"

"Yes," I said. "For a minute, I almost thought I *could* fly."

I started down the hall, expecting to hear his door close. But instead, I heard him say, "Hey, Russell?"

I turned. "What?"

"You're a pretty good dancer."

I grinned, turned, and ran for the elevator. Who'd have suspected that Tom was a human being?

Who'd have suspected that I'd care?

# Chapter Ten

Everything changed abruptly. During lunch break on the following Tuesday, Mrs. Hale showed up at school without warning, her face pale and her eyelids swollen.

"Lottie, you have to come home now," she said.

Lottie stared at her. "What's wrong? What's happened? Is it Dad?"

Mrs. Hale shook her head. "Come, quickly." She touched Lottie's shoulder. "Please, honey."

"I have to get my jacket out of the locker," Lottie said, bewildered.

"I'll meet you outside in the parking lot," her mother said.

"You brought the car?" Lottie exclaimed.

"It was faster," her mother said.

I watched silently as they left. I'd been ready to take

another bite of my apple, but I put it down. I was sure I couldn't swallow.

"What was that all about, do you suppose?" Dolly asked. "Mrs. Hale looked terrible. She'd been crying."

"I hope it doesn't have anything to do with Lottie's dad," I said.

"Her mother said it didn't," Dolly said. "Maybe something happened to one of her grandparents in Oklahoma. She's crazy about them."

I shook my head slowly, miserably. "I hope not." My stomach felt as if a stone had settled in it.

"Hey, Russell," Tom yelled from the table where he sat with his friends. "Where did Lottie go?"

I shrugged and scowled at him. He could be such a clod. Couldn't he see how upset Mrs. Hale was?

I hoped Lottie would come back before school let out for the day and tell me nothing much had happened, or that there had been some sort of mistake. But I didn't see her again, and after school when I stopped by her apartment, no one answered my knock.

I decided to go to the espresso shop and ask Mom. She would know if something really bad had happened. I passed Tom in the lobby, but didn't stop to answer his questions.

Rain had begun falling, harder than it had since winter, but I didn't worry about getting soaked. I couldn't shake the feeling that something awful was going on.

The espresso shop was nearly empty. Mr. Barker, leaving as I entered, looked serious and started to say something, but I rushed past him without speaking. The little boy with him gawked at me.

"Mom, what happened to Mrs. Hale?" I asked when I saw her standing behind the counter, serving two elderly women.

"Sit by the window, baby, and I'll come over in a minute," Mom said. Her gaze flicked away from me deliberately.

Now I really was frightened. I sat at an empty table by the window and watched Mom nervously while she finished serving her customers. One of the waitresses who only worked on weekends was there, obviously called in to take Mrs. Hale's place.

Finally Mom sat down with me.

"Lottie's grandfather died early this morning," she said. "They're flying back to Tulsa—in fact, they're probably on their way to the airport right now."

"That's terrible," I said. My lips were numb. "What happened to him?"

"He had a stroke."

"How long will they be away?" I asked.

Mom shook her head. "I have no idea. Margaret's mother hasn't been very well, and another daughter has been staying with them for several months, helping out. Margaret probably won't want to come right back."

"It's Lottie's Aunt Jackie who's been staying there,"

I said. "She told me about that."

"Well," Mom said vaguely, getting to her feel. "It's awfully sad. Margaret said she'd call as soon as she knows when they're coming back, so in the meantime we'll send flowers to the address she left with me, and let them know we're thinking about them."

"Sure," I said. "Sure."

Two weeks passed before I heard from Lottie. She wrote a letter thanking us for the flowers. But she didn't say a word about when she'd be returning to Seattle.

Dolly got a letter, too, but it didn't provide any more information.

"I bet she's not coming back," I said one afternoon when Dolly was sitting in my bedroom listening to tapes.

Dolly looked at me in astonishment. "Why do you say that? She's got to finish seventh grade. She's already missed two weeks."

"I bet she's going to live with her grandmother now," I said. "She told me about her grandparents' house and how her mother grew up there and all. Maybe both of them will stay there."

"What would your mom do then?" Dolly asked. "Isn't Mrs. Hale her partner in the espresso shop?"

What if Mom couldn't run the shop on her own? She could lose the business. We'd have to start all over again. How many times can this happen, I wondered.

"Mrs. Hale might come back," I said, wanting to believe myself. But I didn't.

That night I sat in my room for a long time, trying to read, glancing up occasionally at the poster of trees. Jimmy patted the book with a furry paw, looking up at my face to see my reaction. But I scarcely noticed him.

It's starting all over, I thought. We're losing everything that matters. Lottie's already gone. Next, Mom will lose the espresso shop. Mrs. Eldrich has finally replaced Mom and Mrs. Hale, so she can't get her old job back. Where will we go this time?

Mrs. Hale came back the next weekend, though, thinner, with dark shadows under her eyes.

The sight of Mrs. Hale alone told me everything I needed to know. "Lottie's not coming back," I said.

Mrs. Hale stripped off her coat and dropped it on the love seat. "Not for the time being," she said quietly.

"That's what Maryanne's been afraid of," Mom said.

The two women sat together at the table, and I fussed over Jimmy's dish in the kitchen while he wound himself between my legs.

"Lottie's always loved Tulsa," Mrs. Hale said. "I thought it couldn't hurt if she finished the school year there and maybe spent the summer with my mother."

I raised my head and smiled at this glimmer of hope. Lottie would be back at the end of summer.

"We'll see how it goes," Mrs. Hale concluded.

I looked down again, deflated. When mothers said they'd "see how it goes," they usually were softening a blow. So maybe Lottie wouldn't be back.

"You didn't have to rush home," Mom told Mrs. Hale. "I've been managing."

I could read Mom's mind. She was worried that her friend might not want the shop any longer. I held my breath, waiting for Mrs. Hale's response.

"I couldn't leave you with all the responsibility," Mrs. Hale said. She smiled a little. "This is the first time I've ever been self-employed. It's a pretty good feeling, and right now I need all the good feelings I can get."

"I'm glad you're back," Mom said. "Everyone's missed you."

"Not Stephen Barker, I bet," Mrs. Hale said.

I raised my head curiously and looked at them. Mom was struggling to keep from grinning. "Him, too," she said. "Oh, I almost forgot to tell you. His little boy's here, staying with him."

"It was bound to happen," Mrs. Hale said. She leaned on her elbows, as I had seen her do dozens of times when they were about to trade gossip. "Isn't his name Cody? What's he like?"

"He's awfully sweet," Mom said. "Stephen's been driving him back and forth to his school in Lynnwood, so the grandmother's been helping out in the bookstore every afternoon."

"Cody will be living with Stephen permanently

now, right?" Mrs. Hale asked. "It's nice he's got that duplex, with his mother right next door to help out with the boy."

"And they've got a wonderful yard for Cody," Mom said.

"Where is Mr. Barker's wife?" I blurted. I knew that my voice had an angry edge to it, but I was tired of hearing this sickeningly happy story about Mr. Barker's son and his mother and his duplex and his wonderful yard.

Mom blinked, a little taken aback. "He's divorced," she said mildly. "And she'd rather not have Cody with her."

I stared at Mom. "She doesn't want her own kid?"

"I'd like very much to introduce that woman to my ex-husband," Mrs. Hale said. "I think they're made for each other."

They laughed again, but I looked away. Jimmy, who had waited long enough for his dinner, butted my leg with his head and cried piteously. I set his dish down blindly.

Mom and Mrs. Hale began talking about the waitresses now, and I wandered off to my bedroom. Outside, I could hear Tom and some of his friends shouting in the street. I pushed aside my curtains and looked down. They were circling each other on their bikes, and then, as if by some prearranged signal, they all took off at once down the street.

I missed Lottie. I jerked the curtains closed and

clenched my teeth together to keep myself from crying. Everything had changed. I needed to talk things over with Lottie, see what she thought of Mom's knowing so much about Mr. Barker and his son, as if their situation involved her.

Lottie was living in a house now, with a big garden. I remembered her describing it. Why should she come back to the Arms?

⤜

Usually I ate lunch at a table with several other girls from the school choir. The table was often full, so one day when Martie, carrying her lunch, came and stood expectantly beside Dolly, there was no place for her to sit.

"Dolly, there's room for the two of us at the next table," she said. "Let's sit there."

I sighed and looked away, annoyed, wondering how Dolly would respond.

"I've already got all my stuff set out here," Dolly said. "Maybe tomorrow, Martie. Okay?"

Martie left without speaking, and Dolly shook her head. "She's a pain," she said. "But sometimes I almost feel sorry for her."

"Why?" I asked.

"She got left out of a party one of the in girls gave, so she's not speaking to them now."

"She should have figured out a long time ago that they didn't want her at their parties," I said.

"Sometimes they invite her," Dolly said. "When

they want someone to flatter them and laugh at all their jokes and agree with everything they say."

I scowled down at the table. Martie annoyed me by trying to push in where she wasn't wanted. Why couldn't she understand what Dolly and everybody else had figured out? If you care a whole lot about something, you never seem to get it—especially if the caring is obvious to other people.

I had lost my appetite, so I rolled up the rest of my lunch in a paper napkin and threw it in the trash can.

"Aren't you hungry?" Dolly asked.

"I'm going to the library," I said. "I'll see you later."

I was beginning to hate middle school. There was too much homework, and the teachers were crabby, and the gym always smelled of sweat, and half the kids weren't the least bit friendly while the other half were pests. Everything was wrong and nothing was right, and I missed Lottie more than I could stand.

I ran out of school as soon as it was over, heading toward the espresso shop. I'd ask Mom if there was anything she needed from the grocery store. Running an errand was better than walking home with Tom and Vic, with Martie skulking behind. Martie was certain to be in a bad mood and ready with a dozen nasty remarks.

The shop was crowded, and I had to wait a moment before Mom noticed me. There was no place to sit, so I stood patiently by the door until she finally hurried over.

No, she didn't need anything from the grocery store or the drugstore, she said. No, she didn't really need anything at all. "Is something wrong, Maryanne?" she asked.

I shrugged. "I've got spring fever," I said. "It's nice out and I don't want to be stuck in the apartment this afternoon."

"Maybe you could go to the park," Mom suggested. A new customer had come in and I could see I was losing her attention.

"Maybe," I said. I left then, before I could give in to the temptation to complain.

Mr. Barker and a boy about eight years old were getting out of a car on the other side of the street. The boy must be Cody, I thought. He looked like his father, thin, with light hair. The boy followed his father into the bookstore.

For a moment I was tempted to follow them, pretend to be looking for a book, and see what this boy was like, this boy whose mother didn't want him.

He's probably a real winner, like Monica, I thought.

I grinned, hoping Cody was like that awful brat and treated his father exactly the way Monica treated her family. Serves Mr. Barker right, I thought.

Mom got home early for her dinner break, and she carried a sack with her. "Come on," she said. "I brought sandwiches so we can eat while we walk. I want to show you something."

"What?" I asked.

"It's a surprise," she said. "I'm afraid it'll be more of a surprise than you'd like, but I want to give it a shot."

"What are you talking about?" I asked as I followed her out the door.

"You'll see," she said. "Do you want roast beef or ham?"

We headed in the general direction of the park, taking a street where the houses were shabby and rundown. One of them, near the end of the block, had a "For Rent" sign on the porch. Mom stopped.

"What do you think?" she asked.

The house was brown, set in an overgrown garden. There were a long row of dirty windows across the front and a sagging porch that ran under them. The steps were splintered. A climbing rose straggled over the uncut lawn, its trellis collapsed on it.

"What do I think about *what*?" I asked.

"The house. It's for rent, see? One of the waitresses told me about it. I called—we could afford it. And there's a yard."

"Mom . . . " I began. I shook my head. "Have you seen inside?"

"Nope," she said. "I didn't want to waste my time if you hated the outside."

I looked again at the sagging porch, the dirty windows. One was even broken and covered with cardboard.

"I hate the outside," I said.

"Okay," Mom said. "I don't blame you. But don't get

discouraged. Sooner or later I'll find something we can afford. You're sure you don't want to see inside this palace?"

I shook my head again. "Let's go home," I said.

By home, I meant the apartment. I had thought any place would be better, especially a place with a yard. But compared to the brown house, the Aristocrat Arms was absolute luxury.

# Chapter Eleven

It was clear that Martie wanted Dolly as her best friend. Martie also wanted me to disappear. To make her point, she pushed between Dolly and me when we were walking in the halls at school, interrupted every time I opened my mouth, and argued shrilly with everything I said.

"It's almost as warm as summer," I said one morning in early May. "I love spring."

"It's cold!" Martie cried. "I was practically shivering on the way to school. Aren't you cold, Dolly? Aren't you?"

"I'm fine," Dolly said. She rolled her eyes at me and shrugged.

Martie saw her expression and renewed her efforts desperately. "Maryanne, will you look where you're going?" she shouted. "Your big feet get in everybody's way."

My feet were the source of much embarrassment, since they were larger than anyone else's, so I dropped behind Dolly and Martie.

Martie immediately lowered her voice to a whisper and hissed on and on to Dolly. She meant to leave me out, so there was no point in trying to hear or asking her to speak up. I sighed noisily. Dolly looked back, but Martie went on hissing like a leaky balloon.

During our lunch break, Martie dominated all conversations at the table. She hated the in girls now, she told everyone sitting there. Dolly was her best friend forever, and always had been. She punctuated her declarations with dirty looks aimed at me and occasionally at the other girls.

"Martie drives me crazy," Dolly said once. "I hear her voice even when she's nowhere around."

I understood completely. There were times when I flinched for no reason at all because I was so accustomed to Martie's skidding up behind me and squawking at me.

There was no cure for the problem—except Lottie. If Lottie came back, then I'd have someone to walk with and sit beside at lunch.

"Why do people act like Martie?" I asked Mom one morning.

"Beats me," Mom said. "Margaret is the find of a lifetime, as far as I'm concerned. She's a wonderful friend, and I know you feel the same way about Lottie. But we can't always be that lucky. For every Lottie, there seem to be two Marties."

The next time I wrote to Lottie, I told her I missed her and begged for an answer to my question: "Lottie, when are you coming home where you belong?"

I got a letter back immediately, but Lottie didn't answer the question. She loved staying with her grandmother, she wrote instead. She even loved her new school.

The next day I learned that Martie had persuaded Dolly to go downtown with her directly from school. Dolly apologized when she realized that Martie had no intention of including me in the plans.

"Who cares?" I said. I slammed my locker door shut so hard it bounced back and I had to shut it again. Farther down the hall, Martie watched and smirked. "I don't have any money anyway," I added, "and I hate wandering around the malls for nothing. I'll see you later."

I hurried off before Dolly had a chance to answer. Outside the school, the sky was clear and blue, and I saw seagulls circling over the park a few blocks away. I liked the park, and I liked lying on the grass watching the gulls overhead, so I slung my book bag over my shoulder and started off in that direction.

The shortest way led past the old house with the collapsed rose trellis. I stopped in front of it again. The climbing rose had leafed out and was covered with tight pink buds. Someone ought to shove it up into place, I thought. It can't live like that forever.

I turned down the cracked, mossy front walk. No one lived in the house, so no one could complain. Blue and pink forget-me-nots bloomed around the porch, mixed in with tough weeds and what I thought might be the foliage of sweet Williams and carnations. Carnations had been Dad's favorite flowers. He loved the sweet, spicy scent. And there were lilac bushes at the edge of the yard.

But weeds were everywhere, choking everything. And the perennials hadn't been divided for years. One bed was full of firecracker flowers, the leaves six inches long already, but they wouldn't bloom, not when they were so crowded.

I pulled out a clump of grass growing where it shouldn't. "There," I told the firecrackers. "Now you can breathe a little, and maybe even bloom. Maybe."

It would take somebody a long time to fix up the yard. But there were such wonderful things growing here that the work might be worth it.

But the house was simply awful. I studied it, scowling. Mom and I couldn't do anything with a mess like that. And all I could see was the outside. The inside was probably worse. Why had Mom even shown it to me? Didn't she want something more like the house we'd had to give up, only a little smaller, since there were only the two of us now?

I left and didn't look back. We could do better than

that. Never mind that the overgrown yard fascinated me.

❧

"Greetings, regards, and cheerio, Russell," Tom said Saturday afternoon when he saw me taking the mail from our box in the lobby.

"Hi," I answered distractedly as I sorted through the envelopes. Nothing from Lottie. Nothing interesting at all.

"You want to go to the beach? On the Sound, I mean."

I stared at him. "What for? It's too soon for swimming."

"I'm not talking about swimming. I'm talking about just looking around, picking up driftwood, stuff like that." Tom, wearing one of his most ragged T-shirts, leaned against the lobby wall and examined a hangnail with more interest than it could have deserved.

"Did you ask Vic?" I asked suspiciously. I had no patience with Vic's silliness and wouldn't go along if he was part of the plan.

"No, I'm asking you." Tom didn't look up.

"Why?" I asked.

"Jeez, Russell, yes or no!" Tom yelled. "Either you want to go or you don't."

"All right!" I yelled back. "I want to go."

He grinned. "Okay, meet me in ten minutes. Bring something to eat if you think you'll get hungry, and money for the bus, and . . . "

"I've been to the beach before," I snapped. "I know what to bring." I stalked into the elevator and pushed the button for my floor.

Tom was an idiot, there was no doubt about that. But going to the beach was a great idea. I'd already finished vacuuming for Mrs. Burke and had nothing to do for the rest of the day.

I called Mom at the shop and told her where I'd be, then packed myself enough snacks in a paper bag to last the afternoon, and kissed Jimmy good-bye.

Tom waited outside in the hall, a black nylon backpack slung over one shoulder.

"Did you bring enough food?" he asked.

"For you, too?" I asked. "No. I only brought enough for myself."

"That's what I meant," Tom said indignantly. "I've got my own food."

"Then let's go," I said. I wondered what had possessed me to agree to go to the beach with Tom. Wouldn't Lottie get a laugh out of this?

The bus let us off half a block from Puget Sound. The wind carried the scents of salt water and seaweed, and the sun seemed brighter here.

The parking lot was half filled with cars. Ahead of us, on the sand, sunbathers lay on blankets and children waded along the edge of the Sound, screaming and kicking water on each other.

"The tide's going out," Tom said. "There'll be more

130

seagulls hanging around, looking for clams."

I wouldn't have known if the tide was coming in or going out, and I glanced at Tom with a small amount of respect. "Are we going to walk up the beach or down?" I asked.

"Let's go north," he said. "We'll run out of people faster." He shifted his backpack from one shoulder to the other. "I brought a lot of stuff for the gulls. Bread and crackers, and some french fries left over from lunch."

"They ought to like that," I said. I had no idea whether seagulls would eat what Tom had brought, but I wasn't about to let him know that.

"Seagulls eat anything," he said.

I had to hurry to keep up with him. We walked past the people sunning themselves, past several piles of driftwood, and around a point of land to a small, rocky beach.

"This is a good place," Tom said. He pointed to a bleached, gritty log. "Have a seat, Russell."

I sat down and watched him take the seagull food out of his backpack. He threw it out on the rocky beach, and moments later a dozen gulls dropped down and began snatching up the scraps. Before he had finished, I'd counted more than thirty gulls greedily quarreling over the food.

When they were done, most took off again, but they circled over the beach as if they hoped Tom could produce another feast. I slid off the log and lay flat, looking up. The white wings were almost too bright to watch, gleaming against the blue sky. And once again I felt as if I, too, could almost fly. Almost, but not quite.

"Do they have homes?" I asked Tom, hoping he'd say that they didn't, that they didn't belong anyplace in particular—like me.

"Sure they've got homes," Tom said. He sat down beside me and pulled out his pocket knife. "Everything's got a home."

That's not true, I thought as I watched him whittle on a piece of driftwood. Tom's such a nitwit. Maybe he thinks the Aristocrat Arms is a home, but I don't. I'll never think that.

❧

I got back to the Arms close to dinnertime and was surprised to see Mom there, sliding a casserole into the oven.

"How come you're here?" I asked, suddenly fearful. "Did something go wrong at the shop?"

"No, everything's fine," Mom said. She set the oven temperature and then turned to face me. "Dinner will be ready in less than an hour. Then—well—I'm going out dancing with Mr. Barker."

My mind was blank. I have to say something, I told myself. I have to tell her she can't keep doing this. That man, that Stephen Barker with his son and his mother and his duplex and his darned yard.

He's not Dad!

She *can't* go on a real date with somebody who isn't Dad.

I licked my lips and forced a smile. "That's nice," I said.

She's too old to have a real date, I thought. Years and years too old. It's stupid and embarrassing for her to go out with that man.

"I'll go take a shower," I said. "I smell like seaweed."

I started out of the kitchen, but Mom called me back. "Did you and Tom have a good time?" she asked.

Mom was making it sound as if Tom had taken me on a date. As if Mom and I were doing something alike. Now there was a dumb idea. What was the matter with her?

"It was fine," I said. "Tom fed the seagulls."

Mom didn't say anything more, so I took my shower. And I didn't cry, not one tear. But afterward I pressed my face into a towel and said, "Why is she doing this to us? She doesn't need anybody but me. I don't want any more changes. No more!"

# Chapter Twelve

"Gimme a dollar."

Monica, wearing a dirty shirt, stood inside the elevator with her grubby hand extended. I'd never seen her smile, unless she'd just done something rotten to somebody. She didn't seem to have friends—which was no surprise. It didn't take much imagination to see how much she had in common with Martie. I didn't know how Tom and Audrey could stand living in the same apartment with her.

I pushed past her and pressed the button for the lobby. "Monica, I heard your mother tell you a hundred times to quit pestering people in the elevator."

"What's your point?" Monica demanded.

"Forget it," I said, sighing.

"Don't you have anything to wear except those old jeans and that stupid striped shirt?" Monica said. "I heard Martie tell her mother that you wear the same things over and over."

"So what?!" I cried, and then hated myself for arguing with the brat. "Just leave me alone, Monica."

The elevator stopped at Monica's floor, and Tom got in. "Monica, Mom's been looking for you! She told you not to leave the apartment." He punched the button that held the elevator at the floor and grabbed at Monica's arm, but she leaped away from him and ran down the hall toward her door.

"Brat," Tom said. "Jeez, Russell, she gets worse every day."

"I know," I said. I figured Tom wouldn't mind honesty.

Tom sighed and then shrugged, as if ridding himself of a heavy load. When he pushed the button again to release the elevator, he asked, "So, where are you going this rainy Sunday?"

"It's not raining," I said. "The sun's shining."

"Just wanted to make sure you had your eyes open," Tom said. "Are you heading for the beach?"

"No, the park."

Actually, I had planned to walk past the old house once more for a look at the garden. But Tom wouldn't understand my interest in the place.

"I'll come with you," Tom said.

I didn't want company. I wanted to have a good look at the fallen rose and, even though it was none of my business, think of a way to get it back up against the side of the house. Grass was growing around it. Before long there would be no way anyone could get it up without cutting it, maybe even ruining it.

The three second graders playing hopscotch on the sidewalk in front of the building yelled fiercely at us when we crossed the chalked squares. One girl picked up a clump of moist dirt from the planter and threatened us with it.

"Knock it off, Mandy!" Tom shouted.

The girl tossed the dirt at my feet and went back to her game.

"Let's go," I told Tom. "This place is a zoo."

"No way, Russell," he argued. "Don't give zoos a bad name."

"I thought you liked the Aristocrat Arms," I said.

"It's better than living in a car."

I expected him to laugh when he said it, but he didn't. He loped across the street and I had to hurry to catch up.

His life was harder than mine. He was crammed into an apartment where nothing ever seemed to get picked up or put away. Even worse, his parents fought. And then there was Monica.

How come real life is so different from television?

"What's wrong with you?" Tom asked. He was staring.

I slapped the tip of a low-hanging branch as we passed under an old maple tree. "Nothing's wrong," I said.

"You look mad."

"I will be if you don't shut up."

"I thought maybe you were mad because your mom had a date last night," he said, smirking.

I turned on him furiously. "What's that supposed to mean?"

Tom held up his hands defensively. "It means your mom had a date with that guy who owns the bookstore across the street from the espresso shop. His name's Stephen Barker—"

"I know his name, you moron!" I yelled.

"He's nice," Tom offered. "He's even nice to Monica. And his kid is sort of funny. He's smart—"

"Like you, I suppose," I said scornfully.

We were approaching the old house. A car was parked on the street in front of it, and I saw with horror that an old man was getting out. He was going to rent it. He'd cut the climbing rose off at the roots and dig everything out of the flower beds, even the perennials.

"What does *he* want?" I said aloud.

"Who? Who are you talking about?"

"Shh. Be quiet." I stopped to watch the man climb the steps to the front door. He had a key. He let himself in and closed the door behind him.

"He's rented it," I said. "He's going to move in and ruin everything in the yard."

"What are you talking about?" Tom asked. "That man? Do you know him? What's going on?"

I didn't answer, and when Tom urged me to keep

walking, I told him to go on alone. I wanted to see what the man was going to do.

"Do you think he's a burglar?" Tom asked. "What could there be to steal? That house is vacant."

The old man came back out and locked the door, then paused by the "For Rent" sign. He brushed it with one hand and straightened it a little, stepped back to look at it, and then left the porch.

Maybe he was the owner. I squared my shoulders and stepped up to him.

"Do you know anything about this house?" I asked.

I had to repeat myself twice, because the man seemed to be hard of hearing. Finally he understood me, and he asked why I wanted to know.

I fidgeted nervously while I wondered what possessed me to start the conversation. "I've seen the sign," I said. "Do you own this house or are you going to rent it yourself?"

"You and your husband here are looking for a place to set up housekeeping?" the old man said, laughing at me.

My face burned and I took a step away from Tom, who was making indignant huffing noises. "My mom is thinking of renting a house," I said, hoping Tom wouldn't spoil everything by calling me a liar just so that he could start an argument.

"Zat so?" the man said. "Your mother can call me about it. My phone number's on the sign." He limped toward his car.

"How much is the rent?" I asked.

The old man stopped again and peered at me from under his thick eyebrows. "Not much," he said. "It's got good wiring and plumbing—"

"And a broken window and the porch is ready to cave in," Tom said.

I turned on him furiously. "Never mind!"

The man reached for his car door. "If your mother's really interested, she can call me," he said.

I watched him drive away. Mom and I would never be interested. The house was awful.

But the yard—it was full of all sorts of wonderful things. They were buried in the weeds, but with some hard work—lots of hard work—it could be beautiful again.

"Come on, Russell," Tom said. "Are we going to the park or not?"

I sighed and followed him. There was no point in looking back at the house. It was impossible. We were better off where we were.

"You know, you are really weird," Tom said.

I punched his arm. "Look who's talking," I said.

"So tell me about your mom's date," Tom said.

I glared. "I want to know how you found out."

"I saw them last night," he said. "He opened his car door for her."

"You mean instead of getting in and driving away and letting her run alongside to catch up, the way you'd do?" I asked.

Tom grinned. "Yeah," he said. "Yeah."

Mr. Barker walked home with Mom that evening after the espresso shop closed. Of course, Mrs. Hale was with them. I'd been leaning over the balcony railing when I saw them coming, so I hurried back inside before they got the idea I was spying on them.

"She's with that man again," I told Jimmy, who didn't care. He was gnawing on an old sneaker, his tail lashing furiously. I sighed and waited for Mom to come in the door.

She was surprised to see me standing in the middle of the living room. "Is something wrong, Maryanne?"

"No. But I wanted to talk to you."

Mom gestured toward the table. "Let's sit down, okay? My feet hurt and I'm thirsty for something that doesn't smell like coffee. Do we have any lemonade?"

"I made some this afternoon." I filled two glasses and put them on the table.

"Okay, so what's going on?" Mom asked after she tasted the lemonade.

"How are you doing at the shop?" I asked. "I mean, are you still having money troubles like you did when you first took it over?"

Mom studied me over the rim of her glass. "I don't know that we had all that much trouble, but we aren't out of the woods yet, if that's what you mean. And we won't be until we've got Mr. Penn paid off, which could take a long time. Why are you asking? Are you

140

worried again? I told you we're going to make it just fine."

"But do you have enough money so we could move from here, maybe have a house again? A nice one?"

"Heavens, no." Mom took a big swallow of her lemonade. "I'm afraid that old brown house is the best we could manage right now, and it's really too awful to be serious about."

I traced a design with my fingertip on the table. "There's not much room here. And we don't have a yard. And there's all the noise and people."

"And you miss Lottie. That makes everything worse."

I nodded. "I don't even know if she's coming back. She doesn't talk about it in her letters, and her mother says she hasn't made up her mind yet. Without her here, well . . ."

"Do you want me to get in touch with the owner of the house I showed you? Maybe if we saw the inside we might find it isn't so bad."

I thought about the shabby house. And I thought about the Castle, the wonderful house I'd daydreamed about. Naturally I would rather move to the Castle.

The kitchen window was open, and we heard Monica outside on the sidewalk, shrieking threats at someone. Mrs. Kingsley yelled at her. Somewhere a baby cried tirelessly. The air was heavy with the scent of broiling hamburger and onions.

"We could look at the old house, I guess," I said.

"Maybe the inside isn't so bad. And the yard could be wonderful. There are big trees in it, and lilacs blooming. You could still walk to the shop."

"It's too dark to see the place now," Mom said, "but I'm taking the early shift tomorrow, so we can look at it after school. How about that?"

"We'll probably hate it," I said.

"Probably," Mom said, smiling a little. "So don't get your hopes up."

I went to bed confused, but a little bit happy. Maybe the house would be horrible inside. But maybe it wouldn't.

In the middle of the night I woke up with a start. I'd been dreaming of Mr. Barker opening his car door for Mom and a little boy. I groped in the dark for the light switch, then sat on the edge of the bed.

Mr. Barker. And his son.

This is stupid, I thought angrily. Why am I worrying about them? They don't have anything to do with me. Nothing at all. It's going to be Mom and me forever, and no outsiders.

The next day Mom met me after school and together we walked to the old house. The owner was supposed to meet us there.

"It's awful, isn't it?" I said when we walked up to the porch.

Mom nodded slowly. "Pretty bad, yes. Maybe the landlord will fix the window and the porch. But what must the inside be like? I'm almost afraid to look."

"The owner said it had good wiring and plumbing," I said.

"Hmm," Mom murmured. She looked around the yard. "Heavens, what a mess. I don't believe even your father could have done anything with it."

"Yes, he could," I said. "Mostly it needs weeding. And the lawn should be cut. I can do those things."

A woman came out on the porch of the house next door, wiping her hands on a towel. "Are you people waiting for Mr. Taylor? Did he say he was coming? He never comes Monday afternoons because that's when he goes to the doctor for his shots."

"Don't you dare laugh," Mom whispered quickly. "He's on his way," she called out to the woman.

"It's not a bad place inside," the woman shouted. "It's got appliances, stove, icebox, washer and dryer. There's even one of those microwave things that make you go blind, if that's what you like."

"That's good to know," Mom called out. "Thank you."

The woman went back in her house and shut the door. I let out the breath I'd been holding. "It doesn't sound so bad."

"You're right," Mom said. "It's got appliances, even one that will make me go blind."

Both of us laughed then, and I relaxed. Maybe this could work. Maybe.

That evening, at twilight, when the scent of lilacs was heaviest, Mom and Mr. Taylor agreed on an amount of rent. It would be less than he had originally asked for because Mom said she would repair the window and the porch herself.

Nobody mentioned the shabby carpet and dingy wallpaper. Or the chipped paint on the cupboards. Even with those problems, the house still looked better inside than we'd expected. But still—it was pretty awful.

Could this work?

When we got home, I went to my closet and pushed my clothes aside so that I could read my crazy writing again. I couldn't leave it there. Mrs. Eldrich was sure to see it when she checked over the apartment after we left. She'd tell Martie—and Martie would tell everybody she knew.

Mom was sorting clothes in her bedroom, getting ready to do the wash in the laundry room. She looked up when I walked in.

"Are you excited about moving?" she asked.

"I will be," I said. "Right now I've got a problem. What should I use to wash my opinion of the Arms off my closet wall?"

She laughed. "Funny, I thought of that, too. Laundry detergent ought to do it. Why don't you add a little to a pan of hot water? I'll help when I come back upstairs."

"I'll do it myself," I said. "I made the mess so I'll clean it up."

But my writing wouldn't come off. I scrubbed the wall over and over, and the ink, which was supposed to be washable, seemed to grow even brighter, until at last I suspected that it could be read clearly in the next room. When Mom came back with the clean laundry, she studied the situation and shook her head.

"We have to paint the wall," she said. "And hope the red ink doesn't show through."

I could practically hear Martie telling the story. "They wrote all over the wall in the closet and tried to cover it up," she'd say. "Isn't that crazy?"

Mom must have read my mind. "I think you'd better scribble over the words so no one can read them, in case paint won't cover them. I mean, it's not that we aren't entitled to our opinion of the place. But this does make us seem—odd."

I looked at her and she looked at me—and suddenly we both laughed. We laughed until we were nearly howling.

"Quiet, up there!" The man in the apartment below us pounded a broom handle or something on his ceiling. "Shut up!"

"*You* shut up!" Mrs. Kingsley shrieked from her apartment. "Shut up, Kirkpatrick, or I'll call the cops on you again!"

Mom covered her face with her hands and bent

over double. "Oh, help," she said. "What will we do without these people?"

"Enjoy life?" I asked.

A few minutes later, we drove to a discount store and bought a can of tan paint and a brush. We were still laughing.

# Chapter Thirteen

There didn't seem to be a way to show the house to Dolly without including Martie, because Dolly couldn't take a step in any direction these days without Martie scuttling along behind. I resigned myself and asked them both to walk past the place with me after school.

The poor old house looked a million times worse with Martie standing in front of it, sucking her teeth and shaking her head.

"I wouldn't live here if you paid me," she said. "The paint's falling off the porch, and the steps are crooked."

"It's got three big bedrooms," I said, hating myself for bothering to explain anything to her. "And there are two bathrooms."

"It looks like it's got rats in it," Martie said triumphantly. "Come on, Dolly, let's go before something comes out and bites us."

Something like *me*, I thought furiously.

"I think it's cute," Dolly said. "Look at that round window upstairs. Is that in your room, Maryanne?"

"No, it's in the upstairs hall. My room's in the back. My window looks down the hill toward the Sound."

"Oh, I'll just *bet* you have a view of the Sound," Martie said. She put on her very best sneer, and I longed to knock it off her face.

"I can see a little bit of the water from my bedroom," I said. Mostly I could see the roofs of houses and, in the distance, tall buildings in downtown Seattle, as well as seagulls soaring above the park, the school playground, and the water. Tom would appreciate the view.

"When are you moving?" Dolly asked.

"Next weekend," I said.

"You have to give my mother a month's notice," Martie shrilled.

I ground my teeth. "We gave our notice, but she can't make us stay at the Arms if we don't want to. Not if we've paid the stupid rent."

Martie looked disappointed. But then she said, "You'll be sorry you moved. This is the crummiest house on the block."

"And we're so glad," I said. "After all, we're used to the Arms."

Dolly offered to help us move, but Martie didn't,

and I was grateful. While the house didn't have rats, it did have mice and I didn't want Martie to know that.

Mom had told me not to worry about them, because Mr. Barker would scatter mothballs around the house and leave them there for a couple of days while the mice ran off to avoid the smell, and then he'd plug up the mouse holes under the kitchen sink.

"He doesn't believe in killing anything if he doesn't have to," Mom had explained.

"Is he one of those dumb vegetarians?" I had demanded.

Mom had said, "No, but he's fond of all sorts of animals, even mice."

"Well, I'm not!" I had lied. "I think the mice should be killed."

Mom had merely looked at me.

Mr. Barker would replace the broken window before we moved in, too. And he'd told Mom he knew a carpenter who would fix the porch for a reasonable amount of money. He would help us move, he would bring over his power mower to cut the grass—apparently he would be everywhere he wasn't wanted, meddling in everything.

Remembering, I got mad all over again.

"Let's go home," I said to Dolly and Martie. "We've looked at the house enough."

"What's wrong?" Dolly asked.

"She's fine," Martie answered for me. "She's just

missing the Arms already."

I snorted and rolled my eyes. Fat chance, I thought.

❧

Rain fell on moving day. If that wasn't enough, the rental truck broke down halfway between the apartment and the house, and Mr. Barker, who was driving, didn't know how to fix it.

But I grinned secretly. So he wasn't perfect after all. Good! I hoped Mom was taking note of the man's serious flaws while she was running back to the apartment—in the rain—to phone the truck rental company and ask for help.

Tom and Dolly showed up early to help with loading the truck. They had trotted ahead to the house to help out when the furniture arrived, and I knew they'd be worried, so I climbed out of the truck and walked to meet them.

I saw them sitting side by side on the porch and waved.

"Greetings," Tom said crossly. "What happened to you guys?"

"The truck broke down," I told them.

"And you're smiling?" Dolly asked.

I sobered. "I've got a key, so let's go inside where it's warmer." I unlocked the door and a strong odor of mothballs greeted us.

"What's that?" Tom cried, clapping his hand over his nose.

I explained about getting rid of the mice.

150

"Who thought that up, Russell?" he asked. "It sounds like one of your ideas."

"Stop complaining and help me open some windows," I told him. "Leave the doors open, too. This is awful. The smell was supposed to go away."

"You hope," Tom said.

"Let's open the windows upstairs, too," I said. "We'll get sick if we don't do something about the smell." I actually hoped, for a moment, that we would get sick. Imagine what Mom would think of Mr. Barker's stupid mothballs then!

Upstairs, I pointed out my bedroom to Tom and told him to look out the window. "Take a really good look," I said.

He did, and turned to stare. "What am I looking for? All I see are roofs and buildings."

I ran into the room and pushed him aside. The rain hid the view of the water, and the gulls were gone.

"I saw seagulls here last time I looked," I told him.

"Hey," he said, pleased. He looked out again. "You're lucky."

I told him to lean out a little and look at the big tree next to the house. "There are squirrels living there," I said. "And sparrows."

Dolly ran in. "The truck's here."

"Let's get started," Tom said, turning away from the window. "It's nice," he said as he passed me on the way to the door. "The house, the yard, all of it. It's nice."

It wasn't, not really. Even with a new window and

mended porch, the house was still old and shabby. But there were possibilities—if you had lots of imagination. And there was the wonderful yard. As soon as the rain stopped, I'd do something about the climbing rose.

While I walked downstairs, I looked around. If we lived in the house for a while—if nothing went wrong, if we didn't lose it—maybe everything could be fixed.

It didn't take as long to unload the truck as it had taken to load it. Mr. Barker drove away with Tom, leaving Dolly to help unpack the things we'd need first. After she left, Mom brought Jimmy to the house and then went back to the apartment for the last time, to give Mrs. Eldrich the keys.

Alone in our new home, I pulled sheets out of one of the boxes and headed upstairs to make the beds. Outside, the spring storm grew worse, and windblown branches rattled against the house.

The doorbell rang when I was halfway up the stairs. "What next?" I muttered. I dropped the sheets on the stairs and went down to the front door.

Mr. Barker's son stood there, wearing yellow rain gear much too large for him. The brim of the hat hung over his eyes, and he pushed it back and blinked.

"Are you Maryanne?" he asked. "Are you Mrs. Russell's Maryanne?"

I was tempted to yell No! and slam the door.

"What do you want?" I said.

152

"Can I come in?" he asked anxiously. He pulled off the hat and looked around.

"I guess," I said.

He blinked again. His eyes were light blue, like his father's, gentle and shy. "I'm supposed to wait here for my dad. He said that after I left Tim's house I should come here and he'd pick me up and we'd finish work at the bookstore and then we'd eat dinner somewhere and then maybe we could go to a movie . . ."

He was going to talk until I grew old and died, I decided. "Come in," I said. "Find someplace to sit down. I'm busy."

"Where should I put my coat?" he asked. Eyes down, he struggled with the buttons, and I realized he was afraid of me.

"On the floor, I guess," I said. "I haven't had time to put hangers in the hall closet."

"I could do that for you," he said quickly.

I looked down at him. "How old are you?" I asked.

"Eight. Eight years and two months and—"

"You aren't tall enough," I told him. "Leave your coat on the floor by the door and don't bother me."

Silently he obeyed. I went back upstairs, humming a little. He was a brat, probably. Like Monica. Maybe even worse. I jerked a bottom sheet into place on my bed and flapped a top sheet over it.

"Maryanne?" The boy—I remembered that his name was Cody—stood in my bedroom door.

"*What.*"

"There's a mouse in the living room and he wants out. He's not big enough to reach the windowsill."

"A mouse?" I asked. "But they were supposed to be gone. Your dad *said* they'd be gone." Oh, joy, the man had failed again! I could hardly wait to tell Mom.

Cody fidgeted. "This mouse is still here. What should I do?"

I sighed. "I'll come down and see."

He was right. A small, terrified mouse cringed in a corner near the open windows.

"We could put something under the windows so he could climb out," Cody suggested. "Boxes, maybe."

"We'll try it," I said. "But it probably won't work."

We stacked two boxes under one window and stepped away, to wait for the mouse's next move. It sat in the corner and trembled.

"He has to have an incentive," Cody said.

Incentive? This baby uses words like *incentive*?

"What did you have in mind?" I asked.

"I guess he's too scared to want food," Cody said.

"Then what does he want?" I was growing more irritated every moment.

The boy pawed his hair. "Maybe we could move over here to the side and then walk toward him real slow, and he'd climb the boxes to get away from us."

"He'll run past them."

"Right." Cody studied the situation a moment longer. "Then I'll go this way and you go that way, and he'll see that he's trapped, so he'll climb the boxes."

Or up my legs, I thought. "Okay, let's try."

We moved slowly and carefully. The mouse watched us. Then suddenly it ran for the boxes, shot up the sides, and out the window into the rain.

Cody laughed. "We did it."

"Good job, problem solved. Can I finish making my bed now?" I asked.

"I could help with that," Cody said.

"No thanks," I told him. I started for the stairs.

I heard him gulp and swallow. I've hurt his feelings, I thought. Well, why not? Nobody worries about hurting mine.

I was halfway up the stairs when I glanced back at him. He was looking out the windows, pretending to care what was outside.

"Cody, you'd better come up and help me," I said.

He ran across the bare floor and up the stairs, grinning. My heart wrenched, almost painfully. Poor weird little kid. His mother didn't want him. He'd have to change schools sooner or later, and I could tell he'd hate that as much as I had. He even looked funny— his clothes were too big and his shoelaces had knots.

"Didn't anybody ever tell you not to run in the house?" I cried.

He stopped and said, "Sorry, Maryanne."

I'm really rotten, I thought. It's not his fault that his father takes my mother to movies.

"Look in the plastic bag in the corner of my room," I told him. "Is my comforter in it? And my pillow?"

"I'll find 'em," he said.

"I know," I said. "I know you will."

When Mr. Barker got there, Cody was sitting in the kitchen with me, eating peanut butter sandwiches and watching a nature program on the TV we had set up on a kitchen counter.

"I thought we were eating out tonight, old man," Mr. Barker said.

"No, I got tired of waiting so Maryanne fixed me something," Cody said without looking away from the screen. "Jeez, Maryanne, look at that lizard. Look at his tail! Neat, isn't it?"

"Yeah, Cody, it's neat," I said.

There were lots of things I could manage to do even when I didn't want to, but saying hello to Mr. Barker wasn't one of them. He stayed nearly five minutes and I managed to avoid speaking one word to him.

Too bad, I thought when the door closed behind Mr. Barker and Cody. But we don't need either of you.

The phone service had been connected the day before, but Mom and I were surprised to hear the phone ring late that evening.

"Who knows our number?" I said on the way to answer it. "Just Dolly and Mrs. Hale." And Mr.

Barker, I added to myself. I didn't want to say his name aloud.

It was Mrs. Hale calling. "I know it's late," she said, "but I've got a housewarming present for you. Can I bring it over right now?"

I looked at my watch. "Are you sure you want to come now?"

"Yes! Is it all right?"

"I guess so."

"Ten minutes," she said, and I hung up.

Mom had taken a shower and was curled up on the love seat in her bathrobe with Jimmy snuggled up next to her. "Somebody's coming over?"

"Mrs. Hale says she has a housewarming present for us."

"At least the rain's stopped so she won't get it wet," Mom said.

Ten minutes later, the doorbell rang. Mom put Jimmy down and answered it.

"Maryanne," she said from the front hall. Her voice sounded strange. "This housewarming present is for you."

Curious, I got up and hurried to the door. Lottie stood in the doorway with her mother.

"Are you done putting away the kitchen stuff?" Lottie asked, grinning. "I'm really good at it." She hugged me hard.

"When did you get here? How did you get here?"

"Mom got me a plane ticket. We wanted to surprise

you, so we didn't tell anybody."

"But are you home for good?" I asked.

"Yes, yes!" Lottie said. "School's out for me, and I wanted to get home so I could go to the last dance with you. So answer me: Are you done in the kitchen?"

# Chapter Fourteen

"What we have to do," I told Lottie and Tom, "is get the rope under the rose and pull it up, then tie it in place."

"Okay, let's get to work," Tom said. "But don't ask me again to help you with your crazy plans. Look at the thorns on this rose! It could kill somebody, Russell." He picked up the coil of rope. "I'll hold one end of this while you two slide it under the rose."

It sounded easy, but even though the grass had been cut away—I had Mr. Barker to resent for that!—the rose still caught at the rope, tangled it, and made the job much harder than we expected. We labored and argued for the better part of a Sunday morning before the climbing rose was finally in place against the side of the house.

"It looks horrible," Lottie said. "We must have done

something wrong."

"It looked better when it was on the ground," Tom said.

"Thanks a lot," I grumbled. "I know it looks bad, but after the canes are tied to the lattice and I've pruned it a little, it'll be wonderful."

"It makes the place look like Sleeping Beauty's palace," Tom said. "I vote that we get that rusty old saw out of the garage and cut the scraggly thing down."

"No!" I shouted. "It's my rose and it stays."

"Jeez, Russell, don't come unglued over it. I never saw anybody act so weird about a garden."

There was no way I could explain how important the yard was to me, so I didn't try. I sat on the porch and brushed my hair out of my eyes. "Let's rest. We can finish after lunch."

Tom stripped off his gloves and dropped them in my lap. "Nope. I'm going downtown with Vic. I told you that a million times already."

"Okay, quitter," I said. "Lottie and I will finish."

"Only because I love you," Lottie said, sighing. "I've never worked so hard in my whole life."

Tom waved and started toward the sidewalk. "See you guys."

"See you at school," I said.

"See you at the dance Tuesday afternoon," Lottie called out, snickering.

Tom took off without answering. "All you have to do is mention the word *dance* to a boy and he runs.

160

How come they don't act like that if you say *food*?" Lottie asked.

I leaned back and closed my eyes against the sun. "I'd just as soon skip this dance and try again in eighth grade. Hey, Lottie, we're going to be in eighth grade! How about that?"

"At least next year most of the boys will be taller than we are," Lottie said.

I looked sideways at her and began laughing. "Maybe not," I said. "We're growing, too. At least my feet are."

"You can fold your toes under," Lottie said. "Come on, let's finish the rose and go eat on the boulevard. I'll treat."

I got stiffly to my feet. "First let's go by the shop and say hi to our moms."

It sounded like a good idea, but later, when we got there, I saw Mr. Barker through the window of the espresso shop and I refused to go inside.

"But why not?" Lottie said. "All we're going to do is say hello to our mothers. You don't have to talk to Mr. Barker. How come you don't like him? He's nice, Maryanne. Maryanne!"

But I walked away, my fists clenched at my sides.

The last school dance of seventh grade was no different from any of the others, except that one boy, fooling around with his friends, fell out of a chair and bloodied his nose.

161

"I don't know if I can handle this glamorous life," Lottie said bitterly. "Do you suppose the royal family will excuse me if I leave the ball early?"

I watched the boy with the bloody nose being led out of the gym by two teachers, Tom, Vic, and half a dozen other fascinated pals. "I know what you mean," I said. "This is the first and last time I'll wear a dress to a dance. After this I'll come in Mom's old bathrobe and my gardening boots."

"Don't forget to leave curlers in your hair," Lottie added.

"It would be better to wear old sweats, the kind with little pills all over and a saggy bottom," said Martie, who had walked up behind us and heard us.

I turned to stare at her. Martie had a sense of humor?

"I dunno, Martie," I said soberly. "I was saving my old sweats to get married in."

After the dance, Lottie and I—and Martie—walked to the boulevard and had Double Devil Delights at the ice cream shop. That night I told Mom that I had actually had a good time, in spite of Martie.

"Absence makes the heart grow fonder," Mom said. "I heard that somewhere. But I'm sure it wouldn't apply to Martie's mother."

"Who'd have thought it could apply to Martie?" I asked.

Two days before school let out for the summer,

everyone watched while Tom received the Student of the Year award.

"Can you believe it?" I whispered. "He's been in detention at least ten times this year."

"He always gets these awards anyway, because of his grades," Lottie said.

"He's a big pain," I said.

"Exactly," Dolly said. "You want to bash his head against the wall and hug him at the same time."

I turned to stare at her. Dolly wanted to hug Tom? She didn't really mean it, of course. Anybody could say something like that and not mean it the way it sounded. But Dolly—and Lottie, too—watched Tom accept his award with bright eyes and big smiles, and I felt odd and left out.

The next day we got out of school before noon, officially eighth graders now. Lottie came over to celebrate on the back porch with me.

I raised my glass of orange pop. "Here's to my report card," I said. "It wasn't as bad as I thought it would be."

"What are we going to do all summer?" Lottie asked.

I thought of all the work I wanted to do in the yard. But that wasn't what Lottie wanted to hear.

"Go to the beach every day," I said. "Go downtown to the big library and the Pike Place Market."

"See the zoo and the aquarium," Lottie said. "Take a ferry ride."

The only shadow in my life was Mr. Barker. Mom went out with him once a week, alternating Fridays and Saturdays, and even though she was always home by ten o'clock, I hated being in the house alone. At least, that was the objection I raised.

"I don't like being here in the dark all by myself," I said at dinner one evening.

"Then why don't you come with us?" Mom asked. "Stephen keeps inviting you, but you always refuse."

I picked at my food. "The movies you want to see are sort of . . . well, boring."

Mom looked past me, out the window to the back-yard. "Maybe Lottie could come over. Or you could visit her. Or I could get someone in. I know Mrs. Noyes next door would come over—"

"I don't need a baby-sitter," I cried.

"Well, she'd be more of a companion, something like that," Mom said uncertainly. "Of course, you could stay with Mrs. Barker and Cody . . . "

"With Cody and his *mother*?" I scoffed.

"His grandmother," Mom said. "Stephen's mother lives in the other half of the duplex, and Cody sleeps over with her when we go out."

"I'm not sleeping over with an eight-year-old boy," I said, deliberately twisting what she said.

Mom set her jaw. "You don't want me to go out with Stephen. That's the real problem."

"It's the house. It makes these noises. And it's so big."

"Not that big," Mom said. "And you wanted to live in a house, so here we are." She faced me squarely. "Maryanne, what exactly do you want?"

I met her eyes—then dropped my gaze to my plate. "I don't want you to go out with him anymore. He's not Dad! Don't you love Dad anymore?"

The silence went on for so long that I wondered if Mom would ever speak to me again. Finally she said, "I'll love Dad as long as I live, but he's not here now. Stephen is good and kind—even to you in spite of how rude you are to him. I like being around him. You are the child and I am the mother, the adult, Maryanne. The time is not going to come when you control my life for me. You are entitled to an opinion, but I will still make the decisions I think are best."

"For you," I said.

"I won't ever do anything to hurt you," Mom said. "I may do things you don't like, but they won't actually harm you. Most of me—most of my life—is dedicated to caring for you. But part of my life is mine."

I got up and left the room. While I climbed the stairs, I hoped Mom would call me back, apologize. But she didn't. She didn't.

I slammed my bedroom door so hard the window rattled.

My thirteenth birthday fell on a Sunday. I wanted my party to be in the backyard, which I'd had cleaned up and weeded, and the weather obliged. The entire weekend was hot and sunny.

I gladly invited Lottie and Dolly, but Martie had to be included. I couldn't see a way to get out of it. I still didn't like her, but she'd been half human recently, and once had even phoned me to invite me to a movie—with Lottie and Dolly, of course. But Martie had been the one to call, and I couldn't stop marveling over it.

On my birthday, we sat at the picnic table under garlands of paper streamers, and after the candles had been blown out and the cake cut, Mom carried my gifts out of the house.

There were more than I had expected. I had only invited my girlfriends, but Tom had sent a long, narrow package with Lottie. And there was one box too big for Mom to handle alone, so Dolly helped carry it across the lawn.

"Mom, what's that?" I asked.

"A surprise," Mom said. "Open it last, okay?"

Dolly gave me two paperback books. Lottie had made me a denim skirt, and Martie gave me a T-shirt to go with it. Tom had sent a carving of a seagull perched on a real driftwood branch, and everyone admired it. His carving had improved—the gull was better than the first one he'd given me.

"He makes beautiful things," Lottie said, gently taking the branch from my hands.

I itched to grab it back, but I opened the big box instead. Mom had given me a bracelet earlier in the day, so what could this be?

"There's a card," Mom said.

It was signed "Stephen and Cody Barker."

I gritted my teeth and opened the box. Inside, wrapped in layers of paper, were half a dozen garden tools in a toolbox, a heavy mat to kneel on, a dark gray gardening jacket with many pockets, and a thick gardening book.

"Wow," Lottie said. "Somebody knows what you like."

Mom said nothing. Finally I said, "They're from Mr. Barker and Cody."

"He said you could exchange anything you didn't like," Mom said.

"I like everything just fine," I said. I couldn't look at Mom. "Cody could have come to my party. We wouldn't have minded him."

"I invited them, but they had plans today," Mom said as she gathered up wrapping paper and ribbons.

That night I put Tom's seagull on my dresser and got out the first one he'd carved for me. The music box was in the same drawer, and I held it in my lap for a long time.

I hadn't had the daytime nightmare for a long time, the one where I forgot for a moment that Dad was dead and I imagined him wandering somewhere, looking for us.

But now I thought of him again that way—

worrying about us, unable to understand why we had left our house. But my imagination couldn't hold that picture of him very long this time. Instead, unwanted, the image kept shifting to Cody lost somewhere, looking for someone, bewildered and afraid.

His mother is rotten, I thought fiercely. How can she not want her own child? I put the music box away and went downstairs.

"I think I'll call Cody and thank him for the presents," I told Mom.

She was watching TV. "The number's in the notebook by the phone," she said without looking up.

I called Cody before I could change my mind. His father answered the phone—I recognized his quiet voice immediately.

"May I speak to Cody, please?" I asked. My stomach seemed to be filled with butterflies. Or bats.

Mr. Barker said, "Hold on, please."

When Cody came to the phone, I said, "This is Maryanne. Thank you for the presents, Cody. The tools are just what I need, and the book is wonderful."

"I picked out the book by myself," Cody said. "I looked at all of the gardening books in my dad's store, and I couldn't decide between three of the biggest, and so I lifted them all and this one was heaviest so I figured that it probably had the most stuff in it, except that the covers seem pretty thick, so . . ."

Good grief, I thought, listening to him. He's not going to run down until my next birthday.

But in the background, I heard something else: Mr. Barker was talking to someone not far from the phone, and she was laughing at what he said.

There was a woman there with Mr. Barker. She sounded young. I pressed the phone hard against my ear.

"I've got to go now, Maryanne," Cody said. "Grandma's here."

I hung up the phone, disappointed. I had hoped for a minute Mr. Barker had a woman friend there, a really important friend. A young, thin friend who didn't have one single gray hair.

I looked at Mom, caught up in the TV movie.

"Mom, do you want another piece of my cake?" I asked.

"Good idea," Mom said, her eyes still on the screen. "But make it small. I ought to lose some weight."

I cut her an especially large and fattening piece of cake, one with a frosting rose on it, and brought it in to her.

"Mom," I said as I sat down next to her. "We're all set here, aren't we? We've got everything we need, don't we?"

"Except decent furniture, a car that isn't on the edge of coming to pieces every time I step on the brakes, a college fund for you, and a few other things like that."

"But we can get those things, can't we? All by ourselves."

Mom turned away from the TV and faced me. "Is this about Stephen? Is he what we're really talking about?"

"No!" I said.

"Yes, we are," she said, and she sounded tired and sad. "I thought you understood."

"We don't need him," I said. "We've got each other. He's not part of our life."

"I think of him as a part of mine." Mom pushed the frosting rose to the side of her plate. "I don't want to argue about this again, so we'd better drop the subject."

I dropped it. I was afraid of what I'd hear if I pushed her.

Mr. Barker took Mom to movies, to dinner, and to someone's wedding. Most of the time he made a big point of inviting me, too. I always refused. The Barkers, including Cody's grandmother, had a picnic with Mom and me at Green Lake, but rain interrupted us, so we went home early. I couldn't stop grinning.

Mr. Barker took Mom to an art gallery and bought her a small flower print.

Mom took him to dinner on his birthday.

Whether I liked it or not, Mom and Mr. Barker spent a lot of time together.

# Chapter Fifteen

One morning I went to the Arms to see Lottie—I
needed to talk to someone—but no one answered my
knock. Dolly had gone on a trip with her family, and
confiding in Martie was unthinkable. Even though
she hadn't done anything awful lately, I didn't want
her to see me upset. Martie loved to take advantage of
people.

I left the apartment building more discouraged than
ever. I had a plan I wanted to carry out that morning,
but I was afraid I'd lose my nerve unless I had somebody with me to back me up.

Paper rattled in the hot August wind and I looked
up. The sign hanging from Tom's balcony read, "Tom!
Take out the trash!"

Mrs. Kingsley's messages to Tom weren't funny anymore. I felt sorry for him, especially since his mother

had gone to work full-time and he'd been made even more responsible for his sisters, walking them back and forth to day care and keeping them occupied until their parents came home at night. Audrey was easy to manage, but Monica was impossible. She ran off every chance she got, and Lottie said Tom was always blamed.

"He picks fights with Mrs. Eldrich about his turn in the laundry room," Lottie had said. "I guess he does that because school's out and he can't start an argument there."

Tom had problems, but so did I. I turned toward the boulevard reluctantly. I'd go ahead with my plan by myself. There was no other way.

I found three customers in the bookstore. Mr. Barker waited on one at the counter. A clerk looked something up on the computer for another. And Tom stood in the mystery section, reading the cover of a paperback.

"What are you doing here?" I whispered fiercely when I got close to him.

Tom jumped guiltily. "Jeez, Russell, are you nuts? You scared me blind."

"Why are you here?" I demanded.

He looked exasperated. "I came here for bread and a dozen oranges. What does it look like I'm doing? Getting a book. This is a bookstore, you dim bulb."

"Your mother left a note for you," I whispered, angry with him.

Tom rolled his eyes. "No kidding. So tell me what *you're* doing here. They don't sell nail polish or hair spray."

I pinched his arm and he jerked away from me. "What's wrong with you?" he whispered ferociously. "You act like Monica!"

"Can I help you two with something?" Mr. Barker asked smoothly. "Ah, Tom, you found that book. You'll like it. Something for you, Maryanne? I've got a new gardening magazine."

Tom leveled his deadliest glare on me. "I'll take this book and then get out of here before I end up dead," he said. He rubbed his arm.

"I didn't hurt you, you big crybaby," I protested.

Tom opened his mouth, but Mr. Barker interrupted. "Come to the counter and we'll ring that up, Tom."

Tom gave me another look and shuffled away, still rubbing his arm. "Jeez," he said. "Jeez."

I pretended to look at mysteries, keeping an eye on the counter. Tom paid for the book and left, giving me one more dirty look. The clerk's customer left without buying anything, and the clerk busied herself in the magazine section. Mr. Barker crooked a finger at me.

Now that the time had come, my ears rang and I felt sick all over. I must be crazy.

"What brings you here this morning?" Mr. Barker said, smiling.

"Why didn't you come to my birthday party?" I blurted.

I could see I'd surprised him. He took a moment to answer, and then said, "The truth is that I knew you didn't want Cody and me there."

"I like Cody."

He let out a breath and seemed a little deflated. "Of course you do. I guess I kept him away from a party he would have enjoyed, then. I shouldn't have done that."

"You had other plans, Mom said," I said.

"I made other plans, yes," he said. "I'm sorry if I offended you, Maryanne. I intended exactly the opposite. But it's not always easy to predict what will please other people."

"Don't do anything to please me," I said. "You don't need to. I'm fine, and so is my mother. We don't need anything. *She* doesn't need anything."

"I won't discuss your mother with you behind her back, Maryanne," he said. His voice was gentle, but his words were hard as stones.

"She doesn't need you," I said.

"She'll decide for herself," he said. His face was red. "Now please excuse me, Maryanne. I have work to do." He turned his back on me.

I ran out of the store.

While Lottie and I sat on the beach on a cool, windy day, I told her everything.

"I can't figure out anything," I said. I lay flat on the sand, watching seagulls in the gray sky.

"Who can?" Lottie said. "Mr. Barker isn't even related to you and he gave you all that stuff for your birthday, but he won't talk to you about your mother. How do grown-ups decide things? Do they get advice from fortune cookies?"

She hugged her knees. "I'm pretty sure that grown-ups are crazy," she said. "I wrote to my dad four times while I was in Oklahoma, and he never once answered me, not even to say he was sorry Grandpa died. Then after I came home, he called and said his wife, that Laura woman with the orange hair, was hurt because I forgot to send her a birthday card. I told him she hadn't sent one to me, but all he said was that I ought to show a little respect. Can you figure that out?"

She scooted down on the sand with me. "There's something wrong with grown-ups," she concluded. "I don't think I'll be one."

We both laughed, but I had an awful feeling that the whole world was swinging out of control.

"I'm not going to be grown-up, either," I said. "What an idea."

We laughed again, so hard that a middle-aged couple passing us began laughing, too.

"This is the most embarrassing summer of my life," I told Lottie. "My mother has started wearing control-top pantyhose and mascara. She looks—she looks—"

"Cute," Lottie supplied.

I sighed. "No, not cute. She looks absolutely crazy. But *he* doesn't think so."

"They could get married, you know," Lottie said cautiously. "Did you ever think of that?"

"No," I lied. I thought about it all the time.

A few days later, I was pulling weeds in the side garden when Mom came home from an early shift and told me that she had news for me.

"I'm going to marry Stephen Barker," she said. "We decided over lunch today. We've been talking about it—and he's worried about you, about how you feel. But you must see how kind he is, how fond he is of you. He's a wonderful man, Maryanne, and we're lucky we found each other."

I sat on the grass, too astonished to respond. Of course I had known it was coming. At least, I'd known it was possible. But now it was happening, and there was nothing I could do. I couldn't have felt more helpless if I'd fallen off a roof.

Mom glanced around the yard. "We're thinking of getting married on the Saturday before school starts," she said. "Stephen and Cody will move in with us and then Cody can start school here. They'll bring their dog, too. Sparks."

"Mom . . ." I began.

"It will be all right," she said. "He loves us, and I love him and Cody." She started up the steps, then stopped.

"Maryanne," she said. "I will always love you."

176

"Sparks?" Tom repeated when I told him. He was sprawled on a park bench, eating an ice cream cone and dribbling a great deal on his shirt. "They've got a dog? But you've got a cat."

"I know," I said. "Can you believe this is happening? Lottie thinks grown-ups are crazy."

"She's right," Tom said. He shoved the last of the cone into his mouth and swallowed.

"Mom and I get along fine by ourselves," I said. "Now I'll have a stepfather and a stepbrother and a stepgrandmother and all kinds of step aunts and uncles and cousins, people I don't even know, running all over the place like mice. We're used to being alone."

"Relatives," Tom said morosely. "That's a bummer, Russell. Relatives fight about everything."

We watched the gulls in silence for a while, and then I said, "I suppose I could run away."

"Oh, sure," Tom scoffed. "Where would you go?"

I sighed. "Nowhere. I wish I could turn into a sea-gull."

"Yeah," Tom said, looking up. "Me, too, Maryanne."

Maryanne. He'd finally called me Maryanne. Was it because he liked me? Well, he'd better not! There was too much of that stuff going around!

"You don't understand anything about anything!"

"Nag, nag, carp, carp," Tom said. He got up and stretched. "Come on, Russell, let's go get something else to eat. I'm starving."

Tom acted as if the only thing that was important was that a dog named Sparks was moving in with Jimmy. Was that how he saw it?

Of course, boys had incredibly thick skulls.

Everything was changing all at once, and I couldn't think straight, so I concentrated on Cody and his dog. A fence was installed around the backyard the day before the wedding, because Sparks might run away.

"He doesn't mind very well," Cody told me as Sparks tugged against the leash, pulling him across the lawn.

The scruffy dog leaped around a lot and barked constantly. Jimmy watched him intently from the shelter of a lilac bush. When the dog saw him and dove for him, Jimmy flattened his ears, but he didn't run off.

"They'll be friends," Cody said with confidence. "If Sparks doesn't wet on him. He wet on Grandma's cat—that's Midge—and Midge got really mad and bit Dad and Dad had to go to the doctor because he got an abscess on his finger and the doctor said, 'Why did the cat bite you?' and Dad said, 'Because Cody's dog raised his leg on him,' and the doctor said, 'Can't you keep out of trouble, Stephen?' and . . .'"

He's going to talk until dark, I thought, looking down at him. "Let's go inside and unpack your things," I said.

"Okay," Cody said. "Come on, Sparks, come on."

The dog wouldn't obey, so I grabbed the leash.

Sparks leaped at me, pawing me with dirty feet.

"He's sorry," Cody cried, terrified. "Honestly, he's sorry. Don't get mad at him!"

"It's okay!" I said. "Get a grip on yourself."

I wrestled Sparks inside, and Cody followed, but he looked upset. "Are you going to punish Sparks?" he asked.

"No," I said. "I won't do anything to him."

"What about your mother?" Cody asked.

I looked down at him again. He was pale under his light tan. "What about her?" I asked.

"Is she going to be mad at Sparks?" Cody asked. "Or other stuff?"

"What other stuff?" I asked. I took off the dog's leash and tossed it on the love seat. "What other stuff are you talking about?"

Cody blinked nervously. "I don't know. The stuff mothers get mad at. You know."

I studied him. "Are you afraid of my mother?"

"No," Cody said. But he shrugged, and the shrug told a different story. He was afraid.

"She gets mad sometimes, but not over silly stuff. She never hits anybody or hurts their feelings on purpose," I said. "Okay?"

"Yeah," he said, but he didn't look as if he felt much better. "Okay. Now let's unpack my clothes."

He ran ahead, with Sparks leaping several steps at a time. I followed, thinking hard. Cody was afraid of Mom? That was really silly.

But then, I wasn't exactly comfortable with Mr. Barker, either. (I was supposed to call him Stephen, but I couldn't.) This man was a stranger, and I didn't know if I could trust him or not. I mean, a box of garden tools doesn't make everything all right.

"Remember the mouse that we helped get out the window, Maryanne?" Cody asked. "Remember that day when we had sandwiches and watched the show about the lizards?"

"I remember," I said as I opened the first of the cardboard boxes that contained Cody's belongings. He'd be sleeping in the small bedroom down the hall from me.

"That was a fun time," he said. He pulled books out of a box and stacked them on the floor, then jumped up and opened his window. "Hey, there's a tree outside my window. Hey, Maryanne! It's got a squirrel in it."

I stood behind him, looking out. He had a nice view of the yard and several trees, and even a corner of the park.

"All I can see out of my window at Dad's place is the fence," Cody said. "This is better. This is *okay*."

"At the apartment, all I saw was the ugly building across the street," I said. "Then somebody showed me how to look up at the seagulls."

Cody leaned out and twisted around so that he looked up at the sky. "I don't see any here, Maryanne," he said.

"That's all right," I said. "You seem like a boy who'd rather watch squirrels. The important thing is that you've got something to watch. Come on, let's put away your stuff."

"Okay, and when we're done we'll go down and fix sandwiches and see if there's a nature program on TV and maybe I'll show you some magic if I can find my trick box and after that . . ."

Lottie and her mother were coming for dinner. Mr. Barker's mother was coming, too. I had promised to vacuum and dust the living room, and here was Cody, talking on and on forever.

"We've got a lot to do," I said. "We'd better get started."

It had been a year since Mom and I had come to this neighborhood to see the apartment. I'd been a stranger with an uncertain future. It was still uncertain, but in a different way.

Cody, fussing nervously with the buttons on his shirt, looked around the room. "Tomorrow I move in here," he said. He wasn't smiling. "And then school starts, and the only kid I know is Tim and maybe he won't be in my class." One of his buttons came off in his hand, and he gasped. His eyes filled with quick tears.

"It'll be okay," I told him. "Give me that—I'll sew it back on for you."

He pulled off his shirt and followed me to my room.

181

I kept a small mending kit in the top drawer of my dresser, and he sat next to me on the bed while I threaded a needle.

"Sorry, Maryanne," he said. "I won't do it again."

I looked up at him and grinned. "You'll lose lots of buttons, but it's no big thing, so quit worrying. Okay?"

"Okay," he said.

We sat side by side in silence for a while, and then he got up and went to the window.

"You sure got a nice yard," he said.

"It's yours now, too." I made a neat knot and snapped off the thread. The button was back in place.

"I can help you take care of it," he said. "There's lots of stuff out there."

"I know," I said, smiling to myself. "Everything grows here."